ROAD HORSE

In memory of
Ginny Harrison-White,
an inspirational woman

JANETTA OTTER-BARRY BOOKS

First published in Great Britain in 2010 by
Frances Lincoln Children's Books, 4 Torriano Mews,
Torriano Avenue, London NW5 2RZ

www.franceslincoln.com

A catalogue record for this book is available
from the British Library

ISBN 978-1-84780-070-1

Set in Olympian LT

Printed in Croydon, Surrey, UK by CPI Bookmarque in April 2010

1 3 5 7 9 8 6 4 2

ROAD HORSE

CAROLINE BINCH

F

FRANCES LINCOLN
CHILDREN'S BOOKS

CHAPTER ONE

The field was almost brown at this time of the year, neither winter nor yet spring. A plastic bag flapped noisily, caught by a barb of the untidy wire fence. Sammy pulled up the zip of his jacket as high as it would go and stuck his cold hands in the pockets.

All the horses were over the far side of the field, sheltering from the wind by the granite wall. Except for Julie. That's unusual, thought Sammy, and he went straight over to her.

"Oh no," he cried, the words tight in his throat when he saw the dark shape near the mare's feet. "My foal, she's not ready to be born yet, it's too soon!"

He sank to the ground beside the crumpled form. The bundle of matted fur, cold to the touch, chilled his heart.

"Dad! Dad! DAD!" Sammy raced back home.

His father appeared from the biggest shed. "Sammy, what's happened?"

"It's Julie, she's dropped her foal and I'm sure it's dead," spluttered the boy.

Sammy's father cursed and set off quickly down the lane, with his son trotting beside him. As they reached the mare again, her drooping head rose and she gave a faint whicker.

"All right, girl, all right, my beauty." Sammy's dad stroked the horse's neck, then crouched to touch the lifeless bundle on the ground. "You're right, Sammy, she's not survived the birth. Probably wasn't even alive when she was born. This is bad news."

Sammy felt a strong arm round his shoulders and he let himself slump against his father, letting free his grief. "It's so unfair. Why did it happen?" he sobbed.

"She's come six or seven weeks early. I don't know why it's happened," said his dad gently. "Could be a problem with the foal or the mare, or...." He paused and his voice got darker. "It could have been some of the town lads stirring the horses up, chasing them around like they've done in the past. That sort of thoughtlessness could result in Julie losing her foal."

"I hate them! I hate them!" cried Sammy.

"What can we do? We must do something, Dad."

His father sighed. "Unless we have a witness who heard something or saw what happened, there's nothing we can do. This field is close to the road out of Brookton, so any ignorant yob and his mates could cause trouble with the animals if they felt like it. We can't be sure, Sammy, we can't know for sure why the wee foal died. You go back home and warm yourself up, while I see that Julie is OK and check on the other horses."

"What about my foal? I've been waiting so long for her, my first own horse." Sammy's tears flowed again.

"What's done is done, son. Nothing we can do now but bury the poor scrap."

🐎 🐎 🐎

Sammy lived in a chalet that his dad had built on a permanent Traveller site. An Inter-City railway line passed by the lower field and an industrial estate with its busy road closed in two of the other sides.

Both Sammy's parents had been born on the road in vardos, the horse-drawn caravans, growing up with the wonderful freedom of life on the move. In those days the adults found work on farms, before legislation by the government made the traditional Traveller way of life impossible. Now they were not allowed to stay overnight in special stopping places or travel in family groups, as they had done for decades. So most had no choice but to find a permanent place to live.

"Sammy?" his mum called from the kitchen, when he kicked off his shoes at the door. "What are you up to, you're going to miss the school bus and you haven't had any breakfast." She was pouring cereal into a bowl with one hand and holding her mug of tea with the other.

"Mum, it's Julie's foal, my foal. It's dead," said Sammy flatly.

"Oh no!" His mum and two sisters cried out together, and they ran to comfort him.

🐎 🐎 🐎

Sammy was let off school that day, and his dad took him in the pick-up to work. Dad was good at a number of jobs, but his main one was landscape gardening. Sammy knew that he was a great help to his dad now he was nearly ten. He could shovel, lift rocks and fetch and carry tools.

"I see you got your assistant with you today, Johnny!" It was Cosher, Dad's friend and workmate. He wore a battered baseball cap and Sammy liked him a lot - he was always joking or telling funny stories.

"How's it going, Cosher?" Sammy asked, settling down next to him on a wooden box and accepting the mug of sweet tea that always started the working day.

The talk was mostly of losing the foal, and Cosher was very sympathetic, as he kept horses too.

"Aw, that's tough, Sammy," he said, putting an arm around the boy's shoulders. "Me an' your dad will have to figure somethin' out for you."

"Like what?"

"Well," said Dad, "the Appleby Fair is coming up, must be less than a couple of months away now. Let's think around that, and see if we can make it there this year."

"Oh YES, Dad." Sammy was excited. "Can I get a horse? Can Billy come too?"

"Hold on, hold on," said Dad, standing up and throwing away the dregs of his tea. "We'll get a little closer to June before you start inviting your mates along."

"Only one, Dad, my BEST friend of all," replied Sammy, jumping up. "Just my best friend, Billy."

When Sammy and his family first settled into their new chalet it meant that he had to attend the local school every day. It was difficult in lots of ways, but the most trouble was caused by some of the other pupils. They would wait for him after school in a group, then taunt and provoke him into fighting, knowing that, as a Gypsy, he would always defend himself. As they outnumbered him, the outcome was inevitable and Sammy would get home torn and bloodied.

His parents visited the headteacher regularly to complain about the beatings Sammy was getting outside school, or to defend the revenge he had dealt out to one or more of his tormentors in the playground. It was a very hard time for Sammy, and things could have got a lot worse if it hadn't been for Billy.

Billy joined Sammy's class when his family moved to Brookton. Billy's father had been killed in a fatal accident with the lorry he was driving.

The two boys became friends almost immediately. Sammy loved the way Billy would clown about and improvise short raps on whatever took his fancy. He was a great ally against the bullies, and together they proved themselves to be a team not to be messed with.

"Sammy and Billy,
we've always gotta grin.
Anybody mess with us,
they know they can't win."

Life changed for Sammy after that. Now he had a special friend who was a Gorgio - not a Gypsy - with a fearless toughness and flashes of insane humour to match his own. Everything became a lot more fun with Billy around.

Yet there were times when Billy would withdraw into dark moods because of his sadness about losing his father. Once he explained to Sammy a little about how he felt.

"My dad said we were a great team, Sammy. We played footie most Saturdays and I miss that so much. He was big and strong, bigger than your dad! It's not fair. Sometimes I just feels all sore inside me.... And me mum still gets upset lots of the time. I hate that. I'll be all right, Sammy, just leave me alone for a while."

Then, perhaps days later, Billy would ride his bike out of town to find his friend at the Traveller site. He loved the horses and the different life there.

It hadn't taken him long to learn how to stay on the horses bareback. And he loved hearing all the stories that his friend had to tell about them.

So when Sammy told him of the possible trip to Appleby, Billy was inspired to rap:

"Sammy and Billy,
two best friends,
they're going up to Appleby,
round all them bends.

There'll be donkeys, horses,
and a few dogs,
racing carts, vardos, fiddlers
and tapping dancers in clogs."

CHAPTER TWO

The weeks rolled by, pushed along as fast as Sammy could make them.

"We'll be sure to take you too, Billy," he told his friend. "Dad hasn't said no, so I'm thinkin' that means yes."

"Yeah, yeah," said Billy, "me mum said I'm bound to be going too, cos I bin a wee angel."

This made Sammy laugh. Nobody could ever think of Billy like that!

"But it's true enough," continued Billy, giving his friend a push. "I've bin helping her every time she ask, no arguing at all."

Because they were a one-parent family, it wasn't possible for them to afford all the expenses of the trip to Appleby, so Billy was doing his best to earn a little spending money for the fair.

The boys were sitting in the field near the horses. It was a warm day, the grass was growing again, and the animals were enjoying the tastes of spring.

"Look, Julie's gonna get her shiny coat back soon. Dad wants her to look good as he's hopin' to sell her at Appleby Fair," said Sammy, adopting his father's habit of standing feet wide-spaced and hands in his jeans pockets.

"Why sell her?"

"As she lost the foal, Dad doesn't want to keep her, as it might be bad luck. He's bound to buy another horse or even two. He doesn't seem to keep a horse if there's a possibility of sellin' it."

"Why's that?"

"That's just how it is. We're gonna trot her down Flashing Lane and see who'll take a shine to her. Then," Sammy continued, "we'll be lookin' for a horse for me!"

"Aw, you're so lucky, Sammy," sighed his friend.

"But you can help me, Billy. In fact I really

need you to help me train a horse on to be a trotter. It's a big lot of work you know, to get a good road horse."

Sammy sat down close to his friend and looked straight into his blue eyes. "Billy, you're welcome to share her just like we're brothers," he said. "We're in this together."

🐎 🐎 🐎

Two weeks later, the boys were sitting on the bench seat in the cab of the horsebox. Mum and the girls were behind them, and Julie was tethered in the back with one of Cosher's horses, Bella. They were on the road to Appleby Fair. Cosher was behind, driving Dad's 4x4 and pulling the big trailer.

The previous evening they had parked up for the night in a small lane, for it was a two-day journey to get to the fair. However, Sammy and Billy were going to take three!

"We must be getting near the meeting place now, Dad," sighed Sammy.

"Yes!" chorused his sisters. "We're nearly there, we're nearly there!"

"Ouch!" said Mum, holding her ears, and Sally and Christine giggled.

Billy piped up next.

"Yes, we're nearly there!
Close to Appleby Fair!
One, two, three days it takes.
We're laden with people, horses and cakes!

"Oh Billy, you make me laugh," smiled Mum.

"About another hour should do it," said Dad. "Just another fifty miles of this motorway, then we turn off and start looking for Nan and Grandad. Just got to be patient a little longer. Julie and Bella are needing a break too."

"I'll ring them when we turn off," said Mum. "But I don't expect they'll answer. They really don't get on with mobile phones."

"There's only the one route they can take from their house, so it won't be difficult to spot a horse and wagon," Dad said.

"A chocolate biscuit for the one who sees them first," said Mum, "and put another CD on, boys, so we can sing along the way."

The last motorway miles seemed to go on for ever, but at last the red and blue lorry left the big road and branched off on to smaller lanes. Cosher stayed on the motorway to drive ahead to Appleby and find a good pitch for the trailer.

Mum could not get a reply from Grandad's mobile, so they all kept their eyes glued to the windscreen.

"There they are!" shouted Sammy, as they rounded a corner.

Close to a tall old oak tree growing in the hedge on a wide grassy verge, stood a brightly painted, green canvas topped vardo. A black-and-white horse tethered on a long chain lifted its head to watch the horsebox park.

Sammy shouted out of the window, "Nana! Grandad! We're here!"

Two figures sat near a fire of gently glowing wood, with a big back kettle suspended over it. The man stood up and said in a raspy voice, "Well, look what the wind blowed in! You lot took yer time all right."

Lots of hugs followed. "I don't even recognise this one," said the lady. She had a weather-beaten brown face and was wearing brightly patterned clothes. This was Sammy's Nan.

"This is my best mate, Billy, Nan," said Sammy, pulling the boy closer. "He's going to the fair for the first time."

"Is that so, wee fella?" asked Nan.

"I've always wanted to, yeah," replied Billy. "Ever since Sammy went and he told me about it."

"And how do you fancy staying here by the roadside with us tonight then?"

"Oh yeah," said the boys together.

"You'll be sleeping under the tarp," said Grandad. "Out there with the beetles and such."

"We both bin really looking forward to doin' that, Grandad," said Sammy, "then tomorrow we can help you pack-up and harness Tina."

"And ride in to Appleby on the wagon," smiled Billy.

"Well that's good, boys. We an' Tina will

be glad of your strong wee selves," chuckled Grandad.

More water was put in the black kettle and Mum got a box from the cab of the horsebox. "Made you your favourite fruit cake, Dad," she smiled, opening a plastic container. "And a nice sponge for you, Mum."

"Well, now you're talkin', lass," said Grandad. "Let's clear a space and set these down."

Mugs and plates were carried from the wagon by willing hands and spread out on a red and green oilcloth. Billy and Sammy helped Dad get the horses out of the vehicle so they could enjoy a munch of grass, tethered not far from Grandad's skewbald cob, Tina. She was excited to see the other two and they called to her. The air was filled with lots of whinnying between the three animals.

The happy party enjoyed the tea, cake and chat around the fire before Dad stood up, saying, "Time to make a move, Joanie. We've still got a few miles to cover."

Julie and Bella were reloaded, the noisy diesel engine started and hurried goodbyes were said. Then the horsebox chugged off around the corner.

"There's a small wood down the lane, lads," said Grandad, pointing with his stick. "Go see what dry kindling you can find, and here, take a bag each to carry it in."

"OK, Grandad," replied Sammy, "Can we take Zip?"

"Hey, Zip!" Grandad called his small tan-and-white terrier. "You want to go with Sammy and Billy?"

The dog knew a romp was on offer and he jumped up and down with excitement, his tiny stump of a tail wagging frantically. All three raced away towards the trees. This was their idea of fun.

The boys found some big ones to climb while Zip busied himself with all the fascinating smells and lots of startled rabbits. Finding wood was easy too - they could have filled several sacks with it. Hungry tummies and the sun going down brought them back, dragging a big bag each of assorted sticks large and small, plus a fallen branch that they managed to carry between them.

"Oh, that's grand, boys," Grandad said. "I think I'll get out my saw and cut up that piece of oak right now. Well done. It looks like you've tired out Zip too."

The dog was sitting with his pink tongue almost to the floor, panting rapidly after drinking the entire contents of his water bowl.

Billy stroked Zip's head. "He was chasing all these rabbits, they were darting everywhere, loads of 'em."

"We don't know why he didn't catch one, Grandad," chipped in Sammy. "There were so many."

"You're getting old, hey, Zip, like me," said Nan with a chuckle. "Now boys, there's supper in the pot for you and then we'll all get some sleep - we've got a big day tomorrow."

"Thanks, Nan, we're starving," said Sammy. "But where we gonna sleep?"

Grandad took them around the back of the vardo, from where he had stretched a piece of tarpaulin over to the hedge.

"There," he said.

"Oh cool," said Billy.

"Yeah, that looks great," agreed Sammy,

looking into the dark interior made cosy with rugs and quilts.

"Can Zip sleep with us too?" asked Billy.

"He'll probably be pleased to," said Nan. "He likes his comfort, does Zip."

Then, after eating two bowls each of Nan's delicious stew, the boys crawled into their nest of a bed, followed by Zip, and nobody stirred until morning.

CHAPTER THREE

"Sammy! Sammy! Wake up, the cops are here!" cried Billy urgently, shaking his friend awake.

"What! What's happening? I was dreaming about this horse, it was mine," said Sammy sleepily. Then he suddenly snapped awake. "The cops! The Gavvers! Where, Billy?"

"Yer Grandad's talkin' to 'em. Come on, Sammy."

The boys moved speedily out from under the tarp and around the vardo to find two policemen either side of the older man.

"Of course, Officer, we'll be off after breakfast," said Grandad stiffly. "We've always pulled in here on our way to Appleby. We've never had any problem."

"That may be so," replied one of the policemen. "But we've had a couple of complaints, so we were obliged to make enquiries. We were contacted by a gentleman who owns the nearby wood. He said that two boys were seen leaving it at 9-30pm last night. There is a prominently displayed notice on the fence stating that it is private property." He paused and looked at Sammy and Billy. "I presume these were the two boys?"

"Well, yeah," answered Sammy sullenly. "But we was only gettin' a bit of fallen wood for the fire; we wasn't doing nothin' wrong."

"I am afraid you were," said the policeman. "If there is a notice stating PRIVATE, NO ENTRY, then you are doing wrong to enter through the fence."

"It was me that asked them to look for a bit of wood, Officer," said Grandad patiently. "The lads had been cooped up all day in a horsebox and they needed a bit of a run around. They're good boys and only climbed a few trees for fun before bringing a few sticks for the fire. As I said, we're just here overnight and plan to leave shortly."

"Well, as long as you don't trespass again, and your stay was only the one night," said the policeman sternly. "I'm sure you are aware that the Criminal Justice and Pubic Order Act of 1994 states that it is illegal to camp on the side of roads."

"Yes! Yes! Yes!" Nan called out in a cross voice. "There's scarcely a person in the country unaware of that wicked piece of legislation. Certainly every Traveller is!" She was standing at the half-open door of the vardo, holding Zip to keep him quiet. "You must know it's the fair this weekend in Appleby," she went on. "The famous Gypsy fair that's been going for three centuries, attracting people from all over the world to see the wagons, horses and ways of Romany life that used to be. Horses take a day to do 15 to 20 miles. They aren't machines you know, they need to stop for the night."

"As my colleague told you, madam," interjected the other policeman, "we are just following up a complaint and making sure you are aware of the law."

"Rules and more rules to enslave us all," retorted Nan crossly. "When I was your age we had the freedom to roam when and where we wanted in peace. These Gorgios today will call the police out to stop the cows mooing!"

"All right, Leah," said Grandad quickly. "These gentlemen are only doing their job, and we'll be away as soon as we can anyway."

"Thank you, sir," said the other policeman, sounding relieved. "We will leave you to proceed with your journey and hope you have an enjoyable time at the Fair."

"Yes, thank you too," replied Grandad, as the men got into their car and drove away.

"Pesky police and their blithering laws," said Nan bitterly. "Well, let's get breakfast underway and be on the road before they lock us all up in jail for the weekend!" She winked at Sammy and they all laughed.

Then they tucked into the tastiest breakfast of sausages sizzled in the flat pan over the fire and eaten between two huge slabs of buttered bread, with mugs of hot sweet tea to wash them down.

Sammy wanted to ask questions about the police visit, but he knew better than to stir Nan up any further, as her temper was legendary.

Mam had told him that his great-great-great-grandmother was a renowned fortune and storyteller who could put the 'evil eye' on whoever crossed her. So they respected her and would insult her at their peril.

The story went that she had asked a rich farmer for some potatoes one cold, hard winter. When he sent her away with a kick, she told him that in twelve months' time she would see him in his coffin. And she did!

Nan told fortunes too, but not as much as she used too.

"Are you telling fortunes at the fair this year, Nan?" asked Sammy in between bites of sausage butty.

"Well, I just might. I'll see how it goes once we're there with all the other folk," she replied. "Your grandad's made a good few willow baskets he hopes to sell."

They put out the stick fire and packed up quickly. The iron cooking pots were hung underneath the wagon and the heavy tarp loaded into a holder at the back.

"Here's a brush each, boys," said Grandad. "Give Tina a smarten-up before we start."

"Yeah, I'll do this side," Billy said, brushing the lovely white-and-chestnut coat of the mare.

Sammy set to work on the other side. "I'd like a skewbald if it's a bright colour like

Tina," he thought out loud, as Grandad got her harness.

"You're narrowing the choice, you know, by being particular about the colour, Sammy," Grandad cautioned. "There's lots of things more important than that."

"Yeah, I know," Sammy replied. "I was just thinking what might be my perfect horse. Plus I had a dream last night that I owned a beauty with a white and burnished red coat."

"Oh, I'd love a white horse, or one of those golden coloured ones," said Billy dreamily.

"Now you are talkin' rare," laughed Nan. "Bet you'd like it to drop golden turds too!"

This made the boys laugh so much they had to stop brushing Tina for a while. Sammy loved being with Nan, as he never knew what she was going to say next.

"You've polished up the brass, it looks brilliant," he eventually said, as he and Billy helped harness the patient horse.

"Of course," replied Grandad, lifting the heavy collar and placing it round the mare's neck. "We've got to look our best for the Fair!"

It was true, the paintwork on the vardo was

as bright as new, and inside Nan had polished all her chrome and brass and the decorated china. The whole vardo sparkled.

"I've got my best frock on," said Nan, twirling her full and colourful skirt. "And look how handsome is my Stan, in his waistcoat, tweed jacket and best trilby hat with a feather. Yer hardly looks a day older than on our wedding day, sweetheart."

Grandad laughed and swung her round, then up on to the vardo. "All right! All aboard!" he cried. "Appleby Fair, here we come!"

Sammy and Billy sat together on the front bench with Zip between them. Grandad was on the left, reins in hand, right leg up, the other down, resting on a support. Nan was on her chair in the doorway.

Zip gave a few yaps of excitement when Tina lurched forward, taking the vardo's weight through her collar as Grandad urged her on.

Billy's face was shining with excitement.

Sammy beamed at him, saying, "Here we go, Billy; you're a real Gypsy now."

And Billy replied –

"Gypsy Billy,
he's on his way.
Sittin' in the vardo
on a sunshiny day.

The Gavvers can't catch us,
Tina's in the lead,
off to Appleby Fair
at one horse speed."

CHAPTER FOUR

It was a fair day with big white clouds and plenty of sunshine. Billy and Sammy each took turns holding the reins and driving Tina. After a while the road got bigger, with more traffic, and Grandad got down from the vardo to walk beside the horse, holding her reins loosely in his hand.

"Hey! Another living wagon in front," called Sammy.

"We're going to see a lot more of them as we get closer," Nan replied.

"Yes, boys, keep a look-out. Carts, drays, and all manner of horse-drawn will be heading for Appleby Fair," Grandad said. "Here comes a big dip in the road, time for a walk. It's harder for Tina to hold the wagon back going downhill than when she has to pull it up the other side."

A small wheel was turned near the driving seat to apply the brakes when they descended a sizeable hill. The boys got out happily enough, and Zip wanted to stretch his legs too.

Soon, they drove on to a dual carriageway with faster traffic and big noisy lorries rumbling past.

"Tina's so cool, isn't she, Mr Swale?" observed Billy, as an enormous articulated lorry thundered by.

"Yeah, she just keeps on dead steady as though she were still on a quiet back road," Sammy agreed. "She's amazing."

"Well, you always get the trust of a young horse first. Handled with patience and affection, you'll be able to train 'em for all sorts of work and situations. They'll want to please you. Just like women!" Grandad chuckled mischievously.

"What's that nonsense you're telling the lads?" cried Nan.

"Well, there's always the exception to

that rule," he replied, winking at the boys. "But I'm talkin' about the right animal for the right job. You're not going to put a racehorse or hot-blooded Arab between the shafts, because they've been bred for different things - competitive racing and showing off themselves and their riders. Cobs like Tina are used for hard work like pulling a heavy living wagon. They come from the cold-blooded types that were bred for carrying knights in armour back in King Arthur's time."

"What! Tina's ancestors were war horses?" exclaimed Billy.

"Could be," Grandad continued. "Those battle horses became the ones to work the land, pulling ploughs and shifting timber. No tractors around back in those days. But cobs like Tina have got all sorts of breeding in their blood to make a good all-round useful animal that can be ridden, driven or even cart-raced too."

"Could she road-race then?" asked Sammy.

"Not really," said Grandad. "They breed those horses specifically for speed – they're a lighter built animal. You'll see the whole range showing off their paces along Flashing Lane. But you know we Romanys like the coloured horses best, so there's a bit of Tina's sort in the mix somewhere."

"You're going to help me find a good one, aren't you, Grandad?" asked Billy anxiously.

"Wild horses couldn't stop me," he laughed. "And there'll be a good few of them tossin' their heads and stampin' their feet as sure as eggs is eggs!"

A couple of hours later, after a break, they were trotting along the quieter roads again, getting near Appleby.

"Look what's coming up behind us," cried Billy.

A small cart was moving at a steady lick and catching them up. Grandad pulled into the side as it sped by.

"Hey, Jack! Jack and Seedy!" Sammy shouted.

The two teenage boys on the cart turned their heads and broke into wide grins.

"Whatcha, Sammy!" they chorused, pulling up their pony, which was wet with sweat.

"You've made it back for the fair then," said the boy holding the reins.

"Yeah, Seedy," replied Sammy. "I'm going to get myself a new horse. Mum and Dad are already there. This is my mate, Billy. You know Grandad and Nan, I guess?"

"Of course! Who doesn't know Fiddlin' Stan and the famous fortune-teller Leah Swale! A very good day to you both," said Seedy rather grandly.

"Good day back to you, lads," replied Grandad coolly.

"Yes, we've seen you often over the years, boys," said Nan disapprovingly. "We know your parents, Stevie and Rose. You've been pushing that wee pony, though."

"It's hard to slow him down. He knows where he's going and can't wait to get there - just like us," said Jack, grinning cheekily.

"Off you go then," replied Nan with a dismissive wave of her hand. "But he'll need a new set of shoes by tomorrow, the pace he's going."

"See you there then," said Seedy, clicking on the pony.

"Yeah, we'll meet up tonight, maybe," replied Sammy.

"You'd be better keeping a good distance from those two, Sammy. They're bad news and so are their family," Nan said darkly.

On the final few miles before Appleby, the road gathered more and more horse-drawn traffic, and a lot of 4x4s pulling trailers too. Nan and Grandad exchanged greetings and bits of gossip with just about everyone they met. Appleby was bustling with life. The roadside was packed with people watching the horses and their bareback riders cavorting around in the river close by a bridge.

Billy's mouth dropped open at the amazing sight of the animals plunging into the river with their riders clinging to their backs as they swam.

"This is where we'll bring Tina and Julie after we've made camp," Sammy told him.

"I don't know if I can do that," replied Billy nervously.

Nan chuckled. "But you have to go and

swim a horse in the river, young man," she said. "That's your Appleby baptism."

The journey ended with a steep hill, and they followed a seemingly endless line of wagons and tired, sweaty horses, plodding up to the camp at the top.

"They call this Gallows Hill, lads," said Nan. "It's where, long ago, poor souls met their end for getting on the wrong side of the law - both men and women! The townsfolk would trot up the hill like it was an entertainment, 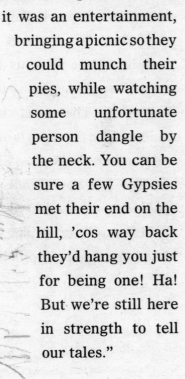 bringing a picnic so they could munch their pies, while watching some unfortunate person dangle by the neck. You can be sure a few Gypsies met their end on the hill, 'cos way back they'd hang you just for being one! Ha! But we're still here in strength to tell our tales."

"What! Kill you for being a Gypsy?" cried Sammy, shocked.

"Oh, yes," said Grandad. "That law was passed in the 16th century when things weren't going too well in the country. People were poor and Travellers were told to leave England or face the death penalty! Gypsies always were a handy scapegoat to blame, and things haven't changed."

"Some of those 'Aga' louts would love to string us up today if they could!" laughed Nan.

"I don't know about that, Leah, but they certainly don't want us livin' anywhere near 'em and spoiling their view - or cluttering up their roads. The car is king and our old life of wandering in freedom is over – we're all labelled and numbered now, just like the cows with their ear tags. But hey! This is Appleby Fair - so we can live as we used to for five blessed days."

"Hooray!" cried Nan, slapping her thigh. "And here we are! Appleby Fair, everyone!

CHAPTER FIVE

Tina pulled the wagon into the field, following the stream of traffic along the dirt track, past lots of earlier arrivals who'd already settled into their spots.

Suddenly, they heard a voice they recognised.

"It's Dad!" cried Sammy.

"Over this way," he waved. Soon Tina was unhitched, and the men rolled back the vardo by its shafts into a space between Dad's trailer and a finely-painted showman's wagon. Tea was brewed, and the whole family demolished cakes and buns.

But Sammy had one thing on his mind. "Can we take Tina down to the river, Grandad?"

"Good idea," he replied.

"You can take Julie too," said Dad. "Guess you want a ride, Billy?"

"Sure." Billy grinned.

"You get on Tina, then," said Sammy, handing him the halter rope. "And I'll take Julie, 'cos she's bound to be a bit lively after a day doin' nothin'."

Billy got a leg-up on Tina and they followed Dad to a big field where lots of horses were tethered, including Julie. Soon the boys were riding bareback towards the river, through the newly arriving traffic.

"This is horse paradise, hey Billy?" said Sammy, as they rode amongst the noisy clatter of hooves big and small.

"I never thought I'd see so many in one place," he replied. "It's fantastic!" And he rapped:

"Horses fat, horses thin,
horses neighing,
makin' a din.
Horses wild, horses tame,
some want to gallop,
that one's lame!"

"Yeah, Billy, tell me more!" laughed Sammy.

Spectators with cameras lined the banks of the river and leaned over the walls of the old stone bridge. The fair attracted thousands of people. Mum said it was impossible to get a bed for the night within thirty miles of the town, as visitors from all over Britain and overseas thronged to Appleby to enjoy the spectacle.

"HEY, SAMMY!"

Sammy turned, and saw Seedy waving to him from astride a horse in the river below.

"You comin' in, then?"

The boys waved back, then took their turn in the queue of animals and riders waiting to get down the slope, where a melee of horses, ponies and riders - mostly boys but the occasional girl too - thronged the shallows.

The air was full of the excited shouts and squeals of the youngsters and the whinnying and snorting of the splashing beasts as they were coaxed into the water to swim.

Julie pawed the shallow river's edge reluctantly, so Sammy flicked her a few times with the rope end, grabbing her mane tightly. She leapt forward into the deep current, submerging him in cold water up to his waist as she swam, her head high and her nostrils flaring.

"WHOOOAAA!" Sammy cried, as Julie lurched out again and shook her body violently, amongst a gaggle of horses being soaped up in the shallows.

Washing-up liquid was used on their wet

coats, manes and tails, to lather them white with bubbles, then rinse them clean so they looked their best for any prospective buyer. The demand was so great for the detergent that supermarkets in the town often ran out during the fair. The tourists loved this ritual and crowded the banks, snapping and videoing with their cameras.

"Your mate can't get his nag into the river, Sammy," said Jack, appearing close by on the small pony that had been belting along the lanes earlier. He and his rider were dripping wet.

"Let's get behind him, then," urged Seedy – he too was totally soaked, and riding a fat white horse with alarming blue eyes.

"We can give him a helping hand," he laughed gleefully.

"Yeah. But careful, guys, Billy's not ridden as much as we have," warned Sammy.

Seedy took his horse behind Tina, who was refusing to go deeper than her knees, despite Billy's efforts.

WHACK! went Seedy's stick on her rump, a split second before Sammy yelled, "Billy! HANG ON TIGHT!!"

Too late! The mare took a giant leap sideways, unbalancing her rider. Then she bucked, sending Billy sailing over her head into the deeper water.

This caused hilarity amongst the crowd, and Sammy laughed too until he saw Billy's angry, wet face glaring straight at him.

"Oh no!" gasped Sammy as Tina spun round, knocked into another horse, and disappeared up the slope through the throng of onlookers.

"Look after Billy, you daft idiot," Sammy shouted angrily at Seedy, and urged Julie after the fleeing horse.

A cry went up from the crowd. "Loose horse! LOOSE HORSE!"

"Out of the way!" yelled Sammy, kicking Julie on to chase after the mare.

"Hold on, boy," growled a big man, grabbing Julie's halter and stopping her. "Don't make a bad thing worse."

"Aw mister, leggo now," exclaimed Sammy. "It's me Grandad's horse – I'll get skinned!"

"Someone will catch her, don't fret," said the man. "You can't go charging through a crowd on a horse. Think about it, lad. Here she comes now."

A couple of young men were riding along the road with Tina in tow.

Sammy apologised to the three of them for all the trouble Tina had caused, and led her back to the river.

On the riverbank was a fuming, sopping wet Billy.

"You all right, Billy?" asked Sammy hesitantly. "Where's those stupid lads?"

"I'm bloomin' wet through and well fed-up!" cried Billy. "Why did yer let those idiots hit Tina that way? You thought it damn funny like everyone else!"

"Sorry, honest I am, Billy. I didn't think Seedy would've hit her like that. Have they gone now?"

"Don't know and don't care," scowled Billy.

"OK," said Sammy sympathetically. "Let's get back."

CHAPTER SIX

There was quite a crowd around the fire that evening, with friends and relatives gathered to gossip and tell tales. Grandad was playing his fiddle, and Mum and Nan joined in at times to sing a song or play the shrill penny whistle. Uncle Dave had a battered case by his side, and Sammy knew it contained the shiny red accordion that he had loved to hear him play ever since he was a little kid.

"See that case, Billy? Uncle Dave's got his squeeze-box in there, and when he's had a few more beers you'll hear some magic music."

But Billy just got up and went to sit on the other side of the fire. He had been in a sulk since his ducking in the river.

Sammy was annoyed too. It didn't seem fair that Grandad had given him an earful when they got back, blaming him for Billy's mishap and Tina's running wild! Only Nan had been on his side, saying that she "wouldn't trust that Seedy and Jack to watch a kettle boil!"

More people arrived as the evening went on. Irish Joe turned up with his wooden board and was soon step-dancing on it, while Grandad and Uncle Dave played him through a fast jig that got faster and faster. Most of the women got up to dance as well, and soon Sally and Christine were spinning like tops and falling down in fits of giggles.

Sammy could not enjoy the fun as he usually did, especially when Billy left for bed as soon as the red accordion began to play. He felt troubled by his friend's withdrawal, as he had so badly wanted the whole trip to be perfect: getting a horse TOGETHER! Now his plans were being spoilt and he wasn't even sure he wanted to be friends with Billy.

Sammy knew that Billy's dark moods were because he still missed his dad, and that the resentment came out in anger that made him hurt people near him. More than once Billy had been suspended from school, and the social workers were regular callers at his house.

So when Aunty Tilly started to sing a sad ballad, Sammy decided to turn in for the night himself.

He also felt he had to say something to Billy.

Billy did not stir when Sammy crawled in beside him, but he wished him good night anyway. After a few minutes he added, "All I can say is I'm sorry for what happened at the river, Billy. I'm sorry I laughed at first and I really hope you're going ter feel better about stuff tomorrow."

Then he fell asleep.

🐎 🐎 🐎

Sammy woke up early the next morning, full of excitement. Perhaps this would be the day he got his horse?

"Billy, you want to see what's happening around the fair?"

"Er, yeah... maybe," murmured a sleepy voice from beneath the covers.

"I can go and have a scout about and come back for you later, if you like?"

"Yeah, OK... see you later," replied the voice.

Sammy pulled on his sweatshirt and found he was first up in the family camp. He walked towards the horses to see what might be going on down there.

Along the track, a few other early birds were preparing for the day ahead, and already the vendors were setting up their stalls.

Sammy passed old metal milk churns, harnesses, kettle irons, pots of every shape and substance. Clothes for babies, sports gear, hats of every kind, grocery stalls, antiques of dubious age and various food stalls from hot-dogs to cream teas, and pancakes. There was even a stall selling the fanciest of gold painted crockery, the prized Crown Derby, pots and plates that could cost as much as a good trotter!

Horses were being groomed and prepared to look their best for possible buyers.

The farrier had a line of horses and ponies waiting, as he filed and shaped the hooves of a big horse with well-feathered legs and its forelock down over its eyes.

Sammy stayed to watch the farrier burn the red-hot iron shoes on to each foot, causing smoke and the familiar acrid smell to fill the air. Then he cooled the shoes in a bucket of cold water and nailed them on to the feet with long sharp nails.

At the water tap were three boys who looked vaguely familiar.

"I'll help you carry those buckets if you like?" offered Sammy.

"Yeah, go on then, take this 'un. They're real heavy and they spill on yer jeans if yer not careful," said a boy about his own age. "I've seen yer before, right? I'm Will and that's Joey and Lee."

"I'm Sammy and, yeah, I recognise you guys, It must have been at another Appleby."

Between them they picked up six buckets and made their way into the field, crossing to the far roped-off corner. All four boys had wet legs from the slopping buckets when they put them down for the thirsty horses.

"See, look at the state of me socks, they're wringing wet now," said Lee pulling a face.

"Me too. These all belong to you, then?" asked Sammy looking at the mixed bunch of horses and ponies.

"Belong to our dad, but the grey pony there is mine, he's called Misty," said Will.

There followed an intense discussion among the boys about the horses, who belonged to whom and their good and bad points.

"I'm up at the fair to buy me first horse," said Sammy. "It's a trotter, a road horse, that I'm after."

"Oh yeah," said Joey. "Plenty of good ones around if you got the money. That coloured mare there has done quite a bit. Fast little thing she is, and I know me uncle's for selling her."

Then all the boys started talking at once, picking out the excellent qualities of each animal before them.

"Hold on, guys!" Sammy held his hands up. "I'm only looking yet. Just seeing what's available before I go up the Flash with me dad and Grandad."

"Fair enough," said Will. "I was only tellin' you what a great opportunity you got to get Jim Boy now. He's already won lots of races, and me Dad's only sellin' 'im 'cos he's got no space for 'im."

"What! You buying already, Sammy?" It was Billy.

"No, but this lot are really keen to sell. Nice to see you, Billy."

"Well, I couldn't stay there in bed missing everything. Didn't think I'd find you, though - it's a big place, hey?"

"Yeah, you've got to find your bearings," Sammy replied. He was delighted to see Billy looking more cheerful this morning.

"We're goin' up Flashing Lane now on the horses," said Joey. "Wanna come?"

Sammy looked at Billy and he nodded back. But the animals had different ideas and trotted away when they saw the halters.

"Let's make a line and corner them," said Will.

So the five boys spread out like gunfighters in a cowboy movie and slowly walked towards

the horses. They edged them into the corner, moving carefully forward to close the gaps, while speaking softly. Suddenly the grey made a break for the widest space between the boys and the others decided to follow.

"WHOA!"

"HOLD 'EM!"

"STOP 'EM!"

Shouts and curses came from each boy as the horses sprinted past their would-be capturers.

A fat little red-and-white pony came straight at Sammy and he held his ground ready to try and grab her. At the last second she swerved sideways, right into Billy.

"Hold 'er!" everyone shouted.

"HANG ON, BILLY!" cried Sammy.

Billy was hanging on to her mane with both hands, trying to dig his heels into the ground. But the pony was too strong for him and shook him off, just as the others sprang at her from both sides and got the halter rope round her neck.

"Got you, madam," said Lee, slipping the halter over her head and fastening the buckle. "Now for the others."

"Good work, Billy," praised Joey. "You was real brave then, an' we wouldn't've got her without you – you OK?"

Unfortunately Billy had fallen in a really muddy patch.

"Aw no, not again!" cried Billy, as he got up, wiping his left side. "I'm covered in wet muck all down..."

Loud laughter from Will interrupted him. "Hey, Billy," he said. "Half yer face is covered too. Yer look really funny, guy!"

Sammy's heart sank, but he thought quickly, saying, "YOU got her, Billy, that's more than I could manage."

"Or me," said Joey "And you made us laugh – good stuff, Billy."

"Come on," beckoned Will, "she's one of the worst to catch, so we'll get the others now."

To Sammy's relief, Billy face broke into a big grin and he rapped-

"Let's go and get 'em, then -
you lot follow me!
Round-up Billy and 'is trusty crew,
we'll catch these horses if it's
*   the last thing we do.*
Look out, Sammy, or you'll fall in the poo!"

That made everyone laugh.

The horses had run through the rope fence in different directions, exciting the tethered ones who were spinning round and whinnying loudly, wanting to be free to join in the fun.

More men and boys arrived to help with the round-up, and eventually the flighty creatures were caught and became calm and manageable again.

"What a carry-on," said a big burly man. "Who's in charge here?"

"We all are, mister," said Will, smiling. "Thanks for yer help."

"Don't know what got into them," Lee joined in.

"You know what they say," continued the big man. "Too many cooks spoil the broth! A load of lads going after them ponies will be sure to make 'em run."

"Yeah, you're right, mister, maybe we're all a bit too whizzed-up ourselves," Will said as he buckled the halter on to Misty.

"Just a minute," said another man, fixing his attention on Sammy. "Aren't you the lad that let a horse loose down by the river?"

"Well, not exactly, mister," said Sammy reluctantly.

"Time to get moving now, guys," interrupted Lee. "Big thanks to everyone for the help."

"Yeah, thanks, see you," the boys cried, setting off quickly before they could get told off again.

Billy and Sammy ran after the three ponies and riders to try and keep up.

"Wait for us!" Billy shouted.

"Get up behind then," said Will, offering his hand to Billy as they caught up.

"I'll have to stand on something," he replied, but Sammy gave him a leg-up, before swinging up behind Lee.

They took off at a trot with Billy's voice
saying -

"Yeah! – ridin' double
away from trouble,
The Appleby Posse
don't need ter struggle...."

"Aw, Billy, you crack us up," laughed
Sammy.

CHAPTER SEVEN

Spectators were gathering along the grass verges of the narrow tarmac road known as Flashing Lane – the Flash! You had to have your wits about you here, as horses were whizzing by at great speed.

Sammy slid off the horse. "Thanks, Lee."

Billy followed suit and Sammy reminded him, "You've got to watch yourself ALL the time here, Billy, 'cos people get killed."

"KILLED?"

"Yes!" Sammy emphasised. "Most of these horses are up for sale an' there's lots of trotters going flat-out to show their paces so people can see what they're made of. Man, they can come along here at twenty to thirty miles an hour!

You get in the way of that and you're mincemeat! Cosher once saw a fella killed on the Flash and the horse had to be shot too!"

"WOW!" Billy's eyes and mouth were open wide. He stepped back to the safety of the fence when, right on cue, a thin black horse driven by a big fat man on a racing cart came clattering by.

"See, it's true, watch yerselves," commented Joey. "We three are goin' this way, we'll probably catch you later."

"See you," the boys called back.

Walking slowly, the boys took in the roadside scenes. There were groups of men gathered in tight circles, as two of them slapped each other's hands in turn.

Billy looked bemused. "What's goin' on, Sammy?"

"If you want to buy a horse, you ask the owner what he wants for it," explained Sammy. "He says his price and slaps your hand, and you say yours and slap his back. Then he says his again and you say yours, slappin' away till the deal is struck - or the owner walks away 'cos he couldn't get the price he wanted."

Billy grinned when he saw the happy conclusion of one of these bartering sessions. A handsome, almost totally white cob was sold, both parties shaking hands with broad smiles on their faces.

"COR! Look at all that money," exclaimed Billy.

"Yeah," replied Sammy nonchalantly. "It's strictly cash only for Gypsies, you can't trust nothin' else. I've got me own bundle here in me jeans. Can't buy a horse without this!" He patted his pocket with a wink.

"Oh yeah?" Billy's eyes widened, "Show us then. How much you got?"

"Enough, I hope, when Grandad and Nan give me what they promised. Come on, we better get back and see what's happening."

🐎 🐎 🐎

Walking slowly back along the lane through the crowds of people and horses, there was something interesting to see every second. A tiny pony no bigger than a large dog trotted quickly by, legs blurring as they pounded rat-tat-tat on the tarmac, and pulling a small cart into which were squeezed to overflowing a plump couple dressed up to the nines.

A mare suckled her beautiful foal in a gateway, while in another a handsome skewbald stallion tossed his head and the mane that flowed down below his muscular shoulders. He snorted, whinnied, and stamped his feathered feet in excitement. A dark man with tattooed arms held tightly on to the bridle. Sammy and Billy looked on in awe, as did all the passers-by with their cameras clicking.

The site was busy with people now and the paths between the stalls and caravans getting muddy. A group of girls approached, dressed up in high heels, short skirts and the tightest of tops. Most Gypsy girls did not get involved with the horses like the boys, but spent their time at the fair parading in their make-up and gold hoop earrings.

The girls giggled loudly as they passed the boys.

"Do you think they're laughing at us?" Sammy whispered.

"I dunno, don't care either. I think girls like that are really stupid," Billy replied.

"Yeah, what kind of twit tries to walk through this mud wearing high heels?" Sammy said, looking after them.

"So what you lookin' at them for?"

"Cos they're so stupid I don't believe it," Sammy grinned.

"They make me feel weird."

"Snap! Me too."

🐎 🐎 🐎

"Hi Grandad. All right?" Sammy asked, when they got back to camp. "Where's everybody?"

"Your dad and Cosher have taken Julie and Bella along to the Flash, Joanie's with your sisters and Aunty Lynda, they're all dolled up in new frocks at the fair, and Nan's got a customer having her fortune told. What you two bin up to, then?"

"We've been up the Flash already, Grandad, we just came back for you and Dad."

"Billy!" said Grandad looking at the side of him all caked in mud. "Have yer chosen to swim in mud today, then?"

"Naw, just fell over, that's all, I'm more or less dry now," said Billy sheepishly.

"Yeah, he's OK. It's getting muddy out there though."

"Well, I intend to stay on my feet. Lads, go get yourselves something to eat, then we'll set off. I'll cover my baskets. I've sold two this morning."

"That's good, Grandad," said Sammy. "There's lots of really nice horses out there, you know."

"I'm sure there are," said Grandad.

"Appleby wouldn't be much of a fair for us Romanys without a few decent horses. And neither would life for that matter," he added, half to himself.

They made their way slowly through the crowd, who milled about to watch musicians, dancers, storytellers, jugglers, magicians, performers of tricks and sellers of wares. Appleby was a festival, a circus and a horse show all rolled into one.

"Feast on it, lads," said Grandad, pausing to look around. "This is as it has been for centuries and as it will be for centuries to come if luck is on our side."

"Hope so, Grandad," said Sammy, but he was thinking about the money in his pocket and what he hoped to spend it on.

"Look, I can see Julie and Dad," cried Sammy, as they came up to the Flash with the sound of horses' hooves clacking loudly on the tarmac.

Dad nodded a greeting and pointed up the road. "Cosher will be coming any moment on Bella."

Sure enough, the dark form of the mare

sped into view, her bareback rider leaning back with reins held wide to give her freedom for top trotting speed.

Heads turned as they flew by.

Then came a racing cart followed by another, both riders' faces mud-splashed from the road. From the opposite direction came the flashing blue light of an ambulance trying to get through the melee.

Cosher rode up on the dancing, sweating and snorting Bella. "There's a cart overturned further along," he said, gazing back the way they'd just run from. "The horse got up OK but the rider didn't look too good!"

A few men crowded around Bella, and one of them seemed interested.

"What you want for her?" he asked.

Well, seeing as this is the finest all-round mare at the fair and I'm not in a hurry to part with her; you can offer me £4000, Cosher said, stroking Bella's sweaty neck.

The man smirked at his companions and stepped forward to look closer, opening Bella's mouth to examine her teeth.

"Why, £400 is too much for this old nag,"

he said dismissively, and walked away with his friends.

"Cheek of the Irish," muttered Cosher, adding a curse.

"A fair price would be somewhere in between, I'm thinking," said Grandad. "Now, have either of you seen a likely horse for young Sammy?"

"There's quite a few nice looking youngsters about," Dad replied, and turning to Cosher, he asked, "Be all right to leave Julie with you while I stroll the lane with Stan and the boys?"

"Yeah, sure, I'm happy here. You lot see what's out there."

The two men seemed to know almost everyone they met. They chatted with lots of people whilst keeping an eye on the horses trotting along the lane and tethered in the spaces and gateways.

"Here comes a good mover," said Dad, as a piebald horse trotted effortlessly by, carrying two boys riding bareback.

"Interesting," remarked Grandad.

"Really nice-looking and fast," said Sammy.

"Yeah," Billy chipped in, "I like the neat blaze on its face, and didn't it have a blue eye?"

"I think both his eyes were blue, how cool is that..." Sammy said wistfully, still looking after the horse.

The rain fell softly, further muddying the lane and the horses. But it was the riders in the racing carts that amused the boys most as they were literally covered in mud from the flying hooves. Their hands, legs, clothing and faces were splattered all over.

When they got back, there was a group of men in tweed hats examining the two mares.

"Here he comes now," said Cosher. "Johnny, there's an interest in Julie."

"Ah yes, Mr Harry Penfold, and what can I do for you, sir?"

"Good day, Johnny, is this your mare then?"

Well, the outcome of that meeting was good for everyone concerned. Julie and Bella were both sold to Harry Penfold, who was a well-respected and kindly horse dealer. The buyer and the sellers seemed pleased with the prices they settled on, and Grandad's earlier suggestion of Bella's worth was spot on.

Yet Sammy was not so lucky. He didn't see the horse he knew would be the special one for him. The blue-eyed piebald stuck in his mind, though, and they all decided that they would look for it tomorrow.

CHAPTER EIGHT

That evening the campfire was sending crackling sparks up into the air, and there was a happy crowd gathered around it, with even more instruments and players than the previous evening.

"I'm for visiting the bright lights and warm pubs of Appleby," Cosher announced, in-between the playing of reels and songs.

"Count me in," said Johnny, and a couple of the other men agreed.

"Can we come, Dad?" asked Sammy, with Billy bright-eyed and eager at his side.

"I've no objection if you want a bit of town nightlife, you two. What do you think, Joanie?"

"Sure, as long as you don't get into trouble, can find your own way back and promise to stick together."

"Yes! Yes! Yes!" the boys chorused.

"How do you like Appleby Fair then, Billy?" Cosher asked, as they strolled down the festival site.

"I like it mega much," grinned Billy, "and I don't want it to stop. I'd never get bored here."

"Too right," chipped in Sammy, as he strode along with his hands thrust deep in his jeans pockets, just like his dad.

"Good!" said Cosher. "That's what I like to hear. Shall we pencil you in for coming with us next time, then?"

Billy looked up at Cosher with wide-open eyes. "Yeah! OH YEAH!"

"Do you agree with that plan, Sammy?"

"I more than agree," said Sammy firmly. "I insist!"

Billy did some dancing steps, singing –

"We're the men on the move
at the Appleby Fair.
We're all in the groove
and we haven't a care."

Appleby was full to the brim with people milling about, and the pubs were crowded to overflowing. Johnny and his friend Moggs went to buy drinks while the others stayed outside to watch the activity on the street.

Cosher was soon in conversation with some friends, as well as waving and exchanging greetings with passers-by.

"It seems like everyone knows everybody else," smiled Billy. "I like that."

"Yes, a massive family," replied Sammy. "So many people here are related. I've got loads of cousins, uncles and aunties - must be hundreds."

"Now look who's here...." The words were spoken by Seedy, who stood there with Jack, each swigging from cans of cider.

"Sammy and his river swimming pal," sneered Jack, "What's yer name now? It's Tilly, right?"

"That's not funny, you..."

Sammy's words were cut short as Billy jumped up and said angrily, "If yer want trouble I'm ready for either of you at any time."

"Ooh! The little water-baby's got a cheeky mouth on him."

"Yeah, and I'm so scared. See me shakin', Jack!"

"Me too! Shakin' with laughin', Seedy."

"Hey! What's goin' on here?" interrupted Cosher. "I don't like the sound of any of you!"

"Just sharing a joke with these two," said Jack. "But they don't have much sense of humour."

"Nothin' funny in your jokes, Jack," Sammy retorted.

"OK, OK, keep yer hair on," said Seedy. "Come on now, let's go, Jack. No fun here."

"Agreed. See you around, guys," Jack said, as he and Seedy sauntered off.

"If they try anything else with me, I swear I'll have one of them," scowled Billy.

"Cool it, Billy, they're just winding you up and besides, they're twice the size of you," Sammy said.

"Those are sensible words, Sammy," Cosher said. "Don't play their game because they'll mash yer mush! You don't want to end up with a pretty smile like mine, now do you?" Cosher grinned wickedly, showing the empty gaps in his front teeth.

"Oh, I can handle them," Billy said defensively. "As long as it's one at a time."

"Come on, Billy, I wouldn't stand by and let you fight alone," Sammy said forcefully.

"What's this?" Johnny asked, looking straight at his son. "Who's going to be fighting who and why?"

"Oh, it's nothing," interjected Cosher. "Just a couple of mindless bozos, trying to stir up trouble. Hand out the drinks now, fellas. I've the thirst of an elephant to quench."

The boys sat down on a handy kerb space and opened their crisp packets and cans of fizzy drink. For a while they watched the mixed assortment of animated people parade by. Then, seeing the adults engrossed in conversation, they decided to check out the area.

"Just going off for a bit, Dad," Sammy said, pulling his father's jacket to get his attention.

"OK, son, we'll be staying hereabouts. Don't go back without telling me."

"Yeah, see you later."

They strolled towards the river through the noisy festival fun.

"Hey look! There's Joey and Lee." Sammy nudged his friend and called out to them.

"Hiya!" Joey shouted back.

"You gotta horse yet, Sammy? My brother has, and my uncle's got this really nice mare and foal."

The four boys got into talk of horses, and they wandered by the river for a while and then sat together on the grassy banks. Time slipped easily away until they realised it was pub closing time.

"Crikey! Best be goin', guys," Lee said, as he and Joey stood up and headed off. "See you tomorrow, p'raps."

Sammy and Billy had almost reached the pub when they ran into Seedy and Jack again. They'd been drinking, and they did not look friendly.

"Oh, it's Tilly, the mouthy little mongrel again," said Seedy, eyeballing Billy.

"Let's move, quick," said Sammy.

"OK," Billy replied.

"On the run, you two frightened bunnies?" Seedy mocked.

"Just what you'd expect from the puny little creeps," slurred Jack, shoving Billy hard into Sammy as they tried to pass.

Billy recovered his balance, turned and kicked the bigger boy hard in his groin.

Jack doubled up, cursing, and Seedy lunged after Billy. He caught hold of his sleeve and yanked him sharply around, right into his fist!

Wildly, Sammy booted Seedy in the backside, then got knocked clean over by a returning blow to his chin.

Jack had Billy down too, and was about to deliver his second punch on the boy's already bleeding face when he was suddenly hoisted off and sent sprawling along the pavement. It was Cosher. He seized Seedy next, and shook him violently, lifting him off the ground.

The next thing Sammy saw, while nursing his throbbing jaw, was a big man grasp hold of Cosher with two huge hands.

Dropping the squirming Seedy, Cosher nimbly spun around, but met the fists of his assailant and collapsed into another man. After a momentary shake of his head, Cosher came back like lightning with a punch so powerful it spun the other man round, and his legs gave way.

Quickly a crowd gathered around the fighting men, so that Sammy could see nothing but legs. Where was Billy?

He pushed himself to his feet and looked beyond the tight circle of yelling men. There was his friend, sitting on the grass. He went over to him.

"You all right, Billy?"

"Think so, what's happening?"

"Looks like the father of those idiots is laying into Cosher. He's massive but Cosh didn't get his name for nothin' - my bet's on him!"

"Uh. Your mouth's bleeding, Sammy."

"Your nose is."

"Not surprised, it hurts like crazy."

"Same here."

Suddenly the crowd swiftly parted, allowing a gap for the big man to stagger out backwards, fall on one knee, then, growling like a rotweiler, rise up and charge back into the circle of men.

"LOOK OUT! The gavvers are coming!" shouted somebody.

Several fluorescent-coated policemen, truncheons in hand, pushed their way through the mass of people.

Sammy and Billy watched in disbelief as the crowd, all in various degrees of intoxication, tried to pick fights with the police, each other; or speedily took to their heels. A fiddler and banjo player accompanied the whole riotous scene. There were even a few step-dancers swaying and tapping their giddy feet while an elderly couple sang, *She'll be comin' round the mountain when she comes*.

But then a big white van arrived, with lights flashing, and several men were bundled into the back - including Cosher.

"Oh no! They've got him," groaned Sammy.

"Look! Yer dad's over there by that lamp post," cried Billy.

"Good Grief! Sammy, Billy! Look at the state of you!" said Johnny, horrified. "Don't tell me you two have been involved in this carry-on?"

"But it wasn't our fault..." Sammy began, and he told Johnny the whole sorry story as the three made their way slowly back up the hill.

"Oh my giddy aunt!" cried Nan when she saw the boys' faces illuminated by the firelight. "Two injured soldiers back from the war, Joanie. And both of you drippin' with blood, and faces swellin' like balloons!"

"Johnny! What's been going on?" demanded Joanie furiously. "You and Cosher were supposed to be looking out for them. Where is HE?"

"Police took him 'cos he stopped them two

lads who set on our two, and then big Stevie Marshall set on Cosher and..."

"And then in came John Wayne, Rambo and the Household Cavalry!" Nan said crossly, hands on hips and looking fiercely at her shamefaced son-in-law. "Why wasn't the fight delayed until morning for the fire of the drink to have cooled down - and the tempers? You know that's our way."

"It all happened too quickly, Leah, I didn't know it was our boys until it was over."

"Well, I hope that stupid bullock Steve Marshall got the thumping from Cosher I've long wanted to give him myself!" said Nan, relenting.

And that set everyone off laughing, even Sammy and Billy, although it hurt them to do so.

Nan clucked and fussed, getting two basins of warm water so that she and Joanie could bathe a boy's face each, adding plasters where they were needed.

"I knew them Marshall lads would cause us grief," she said, "both of them chips off the old numb-skull block. Why, the troubles we've had because of their wicked grandfather. Isn't that true, Stan?"

"A fiendish family as far back as living memory," Grandad confirmed. "Still, they're the inspiration for lots of campfire stories. We can tell a few tomorrow no doubt, but I'm for turning in now and getting some sleep."

Everyone around the fire agreed, and Sammy and Billy led the way to bed, and a good night's rest.

CHAPTER NINE

"Anybody up?" It was Cosher's voice.

"Hey, Billy, you awake?" asked Sammy, shaking his friend's shoulder.

"Yeah... think so," Billy mumbled, rubbing his eyes. "OW!" he said loudly. "What the...?

"Wow, Billy, you gotta real shiner of a black eye."

"Feels like it," said Billy gingerly, touching the swelling. "Hey, your face looks all fat on one side, Sammy."

"It's painful too," sighed Sammy, stroking his cheek. "I just heard Cosher call, it must be well into morning."

The boys pulled on their clothes and got up to find Cosher making a brew.

"Heck! You're messed up, Cosher!" Sammy exclaimed.

"Well, you're not that pretty yerselves, lads. Want a cuppa?"

"Sure, lots of sugar please."

"Help yerselves there."

Gradually all the family emerged from their various sleeping quarters and began dissecting the previous evening's events, as a hearty breakfast was prepared, cooked and eaten.

"Don't care what you say. I'm going to speak my mind to that pesky Marshall family," muttered Nan. "They'll feel the sharpness of my words just like you boys got the sting of their bullying fists!" And Nan set off at a fast pace through the Fair.

"Look out the Marshalls," said Grandad, "My Leah has got her temper up!"

"Are you up for having a look for this horse down at millionaires' row, Sammy?" Grandad asked. "Cos if you want to go home with one, this might be your last good day to find it."

"It *is* the last day, Stan. We're making tracks early tomorrow," Johnny said.

Sammy was shocked. "Aw, Dad, I might not

find the horse I want."

"Now, son, there's going to be plenty of choice as it's the last full day of the fair. People will be wanting to sell before we all go our separate ways."

"Yes, we'll be sure to find a horse suited to you, lad, don't worry. You comin', Cosher?" asked Grandad.

"Maybe catch up with you in a little while," answered Cosher, yawning. "Right now I'm needing a little kip, after that uncomfortable night in the cells."

"OK then, let's be off," Grandad said, leading the way.

They walked along briskly in silence, and Sammy had mixed feelings. He wanted to find a horse, but he was feeling under pressure to get one too quickly, and his head hurt.

🐎🐎🐎

Millionaires' row, or 'down on the corner', was where all the action was going on this morning. Horses and ponies were tethered all around, while the owners and prospective buyers talked business.

The boys followed Stan and Johnny as they threaded their way between animals large and small, and tight circles of haggling men.

"Look! It's that horse with blue eyes," Sammy cried, quickly making his way to a group of three black-and-white horses.

"How much for the wall-eye?" Sammy interrupted the two men who were standing there in deep conversation.

They looked at him and smiled. Then one of them said, "Three thousand pounds."

Dad and Grandad did not say a word but each began to examine the horse, feet, teeth, legs.

"Let's see him in action, then," said Stan.

The younger man jumped up and trotted the horse as much as he could in the crowded area.

"He's perfect, Dad," Sammy said excitedly.

"Costs too much," said Grandad. "I'll give you half your asking price and that's being generous."

"This is one of the best horses at the fair," the man replied defiantly. "He's already winning races and I'm selling him for that price."

Then he and Grandad began a long and animated haggle, with lots of backward hand slapping.

Sammy watched avidly, along with Billy, Dad and now Cosher too.

The tension rose as both men reached the price they wanted to stick to. A crowd of onlookers had gathered to watch the drama and Sammy found he was holding his breath.

Grandad, happy at last that he had got the best deal possible, gave the crucial forward slap of his hand complete with spit, which was matched by the seller.

To finish the deal, Grandad said, "And what do you give me for my luck?"

But just then another man whispered in the seller's ear. He looked behind him, to where some men stood back, leaning on the fence. One of them had a bandage covering one eye, and both were watching the sale intently.

"Oh hell!" groaned Sammy, recognising Jack and Seedy's father under the bandage.

"What's the problem?" asked Grandad.

The man selling was again quietly spoken

to, and after a long pause he looked at Grandad, saying reluctantly, "She's not for sale, as you don't have enough money to buy this exceptional horse."

"What's wrong? You agreed a price!" cried Sammy. "You can't say no now!" He felt close to tears.

"I jes change my mind, I'm not sellin' the horse. FINAL!"

He turned and walked away with the animal.

Grandad cursed. So did Dad.

Sammy was stunned. He looked across at Seedy's father and saw him sneering.

"That no good Marshall. He's to blame for this. I'm sorry, son," said Johnny, putting a sympathetic hand on his son's shoulder.

"Yeah, I should've put his lights clean out!" Cosher said bitterly, looking straight at the figure with the bandaged face. He spat on the ground with gusto.

"I can't believe it," Sammy said flatly – "I'm jus' never ever going to get my horse. Surely you can sort somethin', Grandad?"

"If I thought there was mouse whisker of a chance then I'd try, lad, but it's not going to happen. Too much bad feeling from way back. Come on now, forget that one, there's plenty more to look at."

"But he was just perfect, Dad, isn't there anything you can do?"

"I'm sorry, Sammy, really. I would go over there and offer more money if I thought it would do any good, but the trouble between the

Marshalls and us goes way back, so we jus' try to keep out of each others' way. Looks like the new generation is just the same. Come on now, let's call at the snack bar, then we'll find you another perfect horse."

"Too right, Sammy," Cosher joined in. "Probably was somethin' up with the critter anyway if the owner was connected to Steve Marshall."

Sammy didn't feel at all hungry. He felt sick with disappointment.

"Aw, cheer up now," said Billy, scoffing a triple cheese-burger. "You're makin' me feel bad cos I'm the one who caused all the trouble."

Sammy looked at him, then smiled.

"Naw, man, but you look as if you've bin fighting those idiots again with tomato sauce all over yer face!"

"Oh yeah," said Billy, and he rapped:

"Black eyes and bloody noses,
life at the fair ain't no bed of roses.
Cops put Cosher in the clink
cos some nutters had too much drink.
The perfect horse is not for you -
gotta smile and look for somethin' new!"

CHAPTER TEN

Horses tall, short, stout and slim. Horses pale, dark, bright and dull. Big hairy feet, tiny dainty feet, cropped bristles of mane and forelock, long rivers of mane and fountains of forelock. Whinnies, neighs, snorts and squeals.

But was there a horse here for Sammy?

It was Cosher who was the first to buy.

He spotted a dark stallion that had already won races. "Just the job," he said, entering into the bartering process with the seller and emerging five minutes later as the new owner.

Within half an hour Johnny was negotiating with a tall man in a cowboy hat to buy a nice looking black-and-white mare, which the owner said was in foal.

"Well I'm only going to pay for what I can see, which is one, trim-looking horse, so that's my final offer," said Johnny slapping the man's hand, then making as if to go.

"All right! You're a lucky man, one horse today, two in the new year. I'll do the deal - but only because I like yer face!"

The men laughed and the mare was handed over in exchange for a wad of notes. Then, leaving the newly-acquired animals tethered for collection later, the focus was on Sammy.

A few hours later he was considering three horses that were hopefully within his price range, picked out with the help of Johnny, Stan and Cosher.

Billy was flagging but not about to let on. "Yeah, Sammy, they all look OK," he said.

Grandad favoured a nice yearling colt, but Sammy wasn't convinced. "No," he said, "I think the chocolate-coloured skewbald is a beaut."

Although everyone agreed how handsome and keen that animal was, the men thought he could be getting to the end of his racing life.

Dad had his eye on a skinny chestnut-and-white filly. "She's even got a blue eye, Sammy."

"Yeah, but she doesn't look that good, Dad, she's so thin."

"Not long over from Ireland," said the seller. "I got her in a job-lot and took the fair as an opportunity to sell her on quickly. She needs time I don't have to train on a bit, so she's not too expensive. She's fast, mind, and I guarantee she'll make a great trotting horse!"

"You guarantee it, do you?" laughed Cosher. "Perhaps we could have that in writing?"

Johnny and Stan had been examining the mare as the man was talking her up.

Sammy saw Grandad nod to Johnny, who turned to the seller and said, I'll give you £500 for her, mate.

"Whoa! I'm not giving the horse away," retorted the man

"But Dad...." Sammy got cut off before he could finish when Grandad spoke over him. "Let's see her move, then."

As the man trotted her round, Sammy complained to Billy, "It's as though they aren't thinkin' about me at all. I don't even like the horse. She's got no spark."

"The mare's in poor condition, lads," sympathised Cosher. "But I think I can see why your dad's so interested. With some flesh on her to fill her out and put a shine on her coat, I bet this skinny Minnie will be quite a different animal."

Sammy sighed. "But if they're wrong, where does that leave me?"

"Looks like your dad's gonna buy her anyway, so you can see how things turn out over time," Cosher said, watching the haggling that was now going on in earnest. "Anyway, Sammy, what have you got to lose?" he went on, putting his arm round Sammy's shoulders. "It's not as if there's another horse that's tickled yer fancy – beside the bad luck of trying to get pretty 'two blue eyes' of course – now you have the first option on young 'one blue eye', hey?"

Just then the deal was done, and they turned to see money and halter rope change hands.

Sammy did not know what he felt.

"OK, Sammy," said Dad, looking his son straight in the eye. "I've got a good feeling about this little mare and I've got her for a bargain price. But the last thing I want to do is bamboozle you into something you're set against. Especially as you've been disappointed already over getting your own horse. So I've paid her price and now I'll give you the option whether or not you put your money in and make her yours."

"Can't say that I do want her, Dad. To be honest, I don't fancy her at all!" said Sammy, looking at the filly standing there with her head drooping like a wilted leaf.

"No rush to make up your mind. We can see over the coming weeks if my hunch about her is right or not. I'll give you some time to think about it while she's getting the best food and care I can give her. What do you say to that?"

Sammy just felt crushed. Time was running out and everybody was happy except him. "Right now I wouldn't give my money for this nag, no way, Dad, and I can't see that changing either. Me an' Billy are gonna look some more, right Billy?"

"If you say so, Sammy, let's go on looking," Billy replied, but he didn't sound very enthusiastic.

"It's getting late and I'm done in," said Grandad.

"Me too," said Cosher. "Sorry lads, you're on your own now."

"See you later, boys," said Dad, "Don't buy anything only fit for the knackers."

"Not me," replied Sammy. "That's what you've gone an done already!"

🐎 🐎 🐎 🐎

The boys watched them leave, then Sammy said, "Come on, Billy, you fit? We can go up to Flashing Lane."

"Well, all right, but I'm getting a bit tired. My eye hurts as well."

"Yeah?" Sammy looked at his friend and, seeing his crumpled face, said,

"Just another hour then, my heads aches too. I'll get some chocolate to keep us going."

But despite checking just about everywhere, Sammy could not find a horse he fancied that was within his price range.

The boys trudged back to camp, stopping on the way to look at the new horses Cosher and Johnny had bought, especially the new filly. They found her tethered apart from the others where she had access to some lush long grass. She was tearing at it, and munching with gusto.

"She's really hungry, isn't she?" said Billy.

"Yeah," said Sammy thoughtfully, looking at every inch of her thin body. "Maybe there is a whole new horse waiting to be seen, when Skinny Minnie gets her bones covered."

CHAPTER ELEVEN

"Bye, Grandad, Bye, Nan." Sammy hugged his grandparents before climbing into the cab of the horsebox next to Billy.

"Look after that filly, Sammy, I think she might surprise you," said Grandad.

"She wants cosseting, given lots of treats, just like all us girls. Isn't that right, Stan?" said Nan, winking at her husband.

He nodded and put his arm around her fondly as they waved their goodbyes. "Keep us up with her progress, Sammy!" they called, as the horsebox drove off down the hill.

"I wish everybody wouldn't go on like Skinny Minnie was mine. I keep telling you all I'm not interested in her," Sammy said resentfully.

"Skinny Minnie!" tittered the girls. "Is she really called Skinny Minnie?"

"That's Sammy's name for her, Christine," Dad explained. "The man who sold her said her name was June – he just named her after the month we're in now."

"Skinny Minnie's not a very nice name," Mum said.

"I think it suits her perfect," Sammy replied.

"Me too," said Billy, then he sang,

"*She's SO skinny! She's SO thin.*
You can play a tune upon her ribs,
Hear me now, I'm tellin' no fibs!"

"*Skinny Minnie filly, she should belong to Billy,*" Sammy sang back.

"*I'll have her like a shot, if that's all you got,*" he replied.

"*No, give her to me, if she's not full of flea!*" giggled Christine, which made everyone laugh.

"Skinny Minnie Minx maybe, after the way she played up and wouldn't load into the horsebox," Johnny added.

"She's probably only been through that experience a couple of times," said Mum. "I bet they took her straight off the Irish fields and shipped her over here, poor love."

"Yes, that's probably true, Joanie. There's a lot she's got to learn about life. Like you children, hey?" joked Dad, revving the engine to join the sliproad for the motorway.

The plan was to make it all the way home in one day, as Johnny and Cosher had a big job starting the following morning, digging out and laying a garden for a new client. They could not afford to be late.

The long journey back gave Sammy plenty of time to think about his disappointing trip to Appleby. Yet again he felt fate had cheated him. For so long he had wanted his own trotting horse. He'd grown up watching his dad and Cosher train and race them. The triumphs and setbacks with the horses were part of his family life, and he knew things could go wrong at any time. But if only he could have bought the blue-eyed horse, he would feel so different.

Instead, here was the skinny filly with the

droopy head riding home in the lorry. He felt miserable, and it was a relief when Johnny pulled into a service station and he was able to think about something else.

"Let's give the horses and us a break, hey?" Johnny suggested.

Everyone cheered.

Sammy, Billy and Dad took a horse each and walked them round the grassy area near the car park. They did this two more times on the journey, and eventually arrived home around midnight.

ᴧᴅ ᴧᴅ ᴧᴅ

The following evening Cosher came home with Dad to collect his new horse.

"Well, that little filly's looking better already – what do you think, Sammy?"

"Who? Skinny Minnie, you mean, Cosher? I haven't bothered looking. Your stallion's looking fit though."

"Oh yes, he's got over the journey now and I've told him of the two very fetching mares who are eagerly waiting to meet him,"

Cosher laughed.

Later, Dad asked Sammy if he wanted to give him a hand with the new horses.

But Sammy declined. "No," he said. "I've arranged to meet Billy round his house 'cos we're going to the skateboard park. See you." And he headed off as quickly as he could.

🐎 🐎 🐎

For the next few weeks Sammy avoided the fields and horses altogether, He spent his time round at Billy's house and with some other friends. Horses were OUT! Whenever Dad started to talk about anything to do with them, he changed the subject or didn't reply.

Then one afternoon he and Billy came home to find his dad grooming a horse in the front yard.

"WOW!" Sammy exclaimed, admiring the fine-looking animal. "Is that really Skinny Minnie, Dad?"

"Indeed it is. She's improved no end, hasn't she?"

"I'll say. I hardly recognised her. She's

filled out and her coat's all smooth and shiny," Billy agreed. "She even looks bigger."

"That's because she's not hanging her head like she was when I bought her," Johnny said, stroking her neck. "I'm going to teach her a few basic things if you two want to help me."

"We were going to play on the computer, but yes, I'd like to, Dad. What do you think, Billy?"

"Suppose so, but can we play those games after, so I can pulverise those war lords?"

"Sure," replied Sammy, but already he could think only about the filly, as he tenderly played with her soft nose.

"Can you pass me the bridle, Billy?" asked Johnny.

"It's got a funny bit, hasn't it?" he asked, as he handed it over.

"It's a mouthing bit," said Johnny. "Those keys are for her to play with – a bit of entertainment for her! Here, Sammy, you put the bridle on."

After a little persuasion Sammy eased the bit gently into her mouth, then carefully got the bridle's leather straps over her ears, with Johnny's help.

"That wasn't a problem. Good work, Sammy," his father smiled.

"She's crunching as though she's going to break that bit, or her teeth!" Billy sounded worried.

"No, she's just wondering what it is and playing about with the keys," Johnny laughed.

"I thought horses bucked and kicked and acted really wild when they were being broken in," said Billy, surprised.

"Not a good way at all son, that's just what the movies would have you believe. But if you have a sweetheart like this youngster all you need is patience and kindness," Johnny

explained, as he ran his hands over her back and legs.

Sammy led the filly round whilst talking to her and enjoying the rattle of her teeth on the metal.

"Can I have a turn, Sammy?"

"Yeah, just hold her confidently," his friend replied as he handed over the halter rope.

They took her up to the field and took turns starting, stopping and walking the horse round a small area.

After an hour Johnny called a halt. "That's enough for now," he said, "but we'll carry on like this for a few days until she's used to it. Then in a week's time we can introduce some more harness."

"OK, Dad, I'd like to help you again." Then, turning to Billy he said, "Come on, I'm gonna massacre you in this game."

"No chance!" Billy replied as they disappeared inside the house.

Later that evening, Sammy went to the field and watched Skinny Minnie munching the summer grass. He walked towards her, but she snorted and trotted away, her head and tail held high.

"Even your raggedy tail's growing, Minnie," he called after her. Then he murmured to himself, "No wonder you run away from me. I've ignored you since we got back, but you are going to get to know me now, I promise."

CHAPTER TWELVE

Every evening when Dad got home, Sammy would be waiting to go down to the field with him. He made sure he always had some carrots for the filly, so by the end of the week she came when he called her, then tried to delve into his pockets with her mobile muzzle till she found them.

"Hey! Easy girl, you'll rip my clothes!" he had to say one time.

"I thought she was going to pull your jacket off," said Billy, worried.

"Minnie's looking forward to seeing you now," smiled Johnny. "I think she's rather partial to carrots."

"Yeah, they're not bad, I never tried them this way before," said Billy, taking another bite of one himself.

"Hey! Lay off scoffing her carrots, Billy, fetch yer own," Sammy said.

"OK, I'm just getting into the mood," he grinned, letting Minnie have the rest of it.

"Today we're putting the pad and crupper on Minnie, so all attention on that, please, lads," Johnny stated firmly.

As Sammy tightened the girth, the horse began to fret, tossing her head and prancing on the spot.

"Don't fasten it too tight, Sammy,"

"No, she doesn't like it at all," he replied, as the filly spun half round and kicked up her heels.

"OWWW!" yelled Billy. "She's stood on me TOES!"

"Keep out of her way, boy. This is all new and strange to her and we can't predict how she'll behave." Johnny sounded annoyed.

Billy hobbled away and sat down to take off his trainer and nurse his toes.

"You all right, Billy?"

"Yeah, I don't think they're broken - just bent." He smiled wanly at his friend. "Think I'll go home though, and see you tomorrow."

"I guess that's the best thing to do. Minnie seems a bit wound-up today. See you at school."

🐎 🐎 🐎

Day by day, with a lot of coaxing, reassurance and carrots, Minnie got used to the strange straps that were fastened to parts of her body and would walk quietly around with Sammy leading her. Cosher was coming to visit this afternoon, and Billy too, after keeping away for a few days after the mishap with his toes.

"How's the little lady doing, then?" Cosher asked.

"Very well. She's a bit nervous at some things, but we're really pleased with how she's coming on," said Johnny.

"Today we're lungeing her, and then maybe we'll put the sidelines on in a couple of days," Sammy said enthusiastically. Then he added, "She's well smart, you know, Cosher."

"Is that so, Sammy? Does that mean perhaps that you're interested in owning her after all?" Cosher winked at Johnny.

"Could well be, if she keeps doing as good as she is."

"But you told me you've definitely decided to have her," said Billy.

Sammy frowned. "Well, yeah," he said, embarrassed. "But I just haven't told anybody else yet, Billy."

"Perhaps it's 'make your mind up' time, son. Shall we talk money?" Johnny asked.

"Mmm..." Sammy paused, then said, "Hang on a minute."

He ran back to the chalet and rushed to his room. Opening a drawer he took out a woolly sock and from it a bundle of notes kept tightly bound by many elastic bands. Stuffing it into his pocket, he was soon hastily on his way back out.

"What's up, Sammy?" asked Christine.

"Tell you later."

"SAMMY! Has something happened?" Mum looked worried and grasped his arm.

"No, Mum, but it's about to happen. I'm

going to buy Skinny Minnie - so let me go. Dad's waiting."

"Oh, good!" she cried, releasing her grip and letting Sammy dash out the door, before hurrying after him with Christine and Sally.

Breathing hard, Sammy stood opposite his father, feet apart and shoulders straight. "Here it is, six hundred and twenty pounds for the skewbald filly," he said taking the bundle of money from his pocket. "My first and only offer, take it or leave it!"

Johnny scratched his head, sighed, looked at the horse, then straight at his son. "Your only offer?"

Sammy did not blink nor waver. "My one and only offer."

There was a long pause as Johnny thought about it, and rubbed his chin. Then, looking up, he said, "Well, son, I think I might accept your offer."

They slapped their right hands together before the money was handed over.

"What'll you give me for my luck?" Sammy asked.

Johnny peeled off one of the twenty-pound

notes and gave it back. Then the two spat on their right palms and slapped them together again.

The deal was done!

"Whoa hey!" whooped Billy, as father and son broke into big smiles.

Cosher patted Sammy on the back and said grandly, "Congratulations, a wise decision, young man. You've bought yourself one fine-looking horse."

Mum couldn't help giving her boy a big hug, and the girls jumped up and down with excitement.

Billy improvised on the spot....

"Skinny Minnie was a dud,
young Sammy said, 'NO WAY!'
But it only took a few short weeks
an' Minnie grew so smart and sleek.
Said Sammy, 'Dad, here's all my money,
I jus' gotta have that honey!'"

They all laughed at Billy's rap, and Cosher asked him to say it again so he could join in and do a short step-dance.

Minnie sensed the excitement, snorted her approval and danced a few steps too, as Sammy stroked her neck.

"Here's the next important thing," he said to them all. "Her name's not Skinny Minnie any more. She's not skinny and I just love how her colouring splits her face in two - red-brown one side and white the other. So I'm going to call her Two-Face."

"*Two-Face, Two-Face, you bet she's gonna race,*" chipped in Billy. "Yeah, that's a great name, Sammy."

"Sounds fine to me," said Dad.

"A good Gypsy name," said Mum.

"Yes, it suits her well," Cosher approved.

🐎 🐎 🐎

That week the lungeing went smoothly, and Two-Face responded well to her new owner. Billy rode over most evenings on his bike to take his turn helping out with the filly's training.

Sammy couldn't think about anything except Two-Face, his Two-Face. He was out with her every evening until bedtime and up early to enjoy her company before school.

Soon the summer holidays arrived so all his attention could be lavished on his beautiful chestnut and white filly.

The training continued most evenings. First the sidelines were put on, to get Two-Face used to having to answer to the feel of the bit. Then, gradually, as she seemed happy with it all, they were tightened up.

Next Johnny attached the long-reins from the bit, through the tugs on the pad and gave the rein endings to Sammy. "I'll lead her quietly round the field," he said, "and you just follow on, keeping a light contact."

"These long-reins are really winding her up, Dad. I can only just hold her,"

Sammy said, as the horse gave small kicks and tossed her head.

"Don't worry, I've got her... whoooooa!"

Two-Face suddenly threw up her head and broke away from Johnny, pulling the long-reins out of Sammy's hands. She spurted off at full speed across the field, bucking wildly.

"Sorry, Dad, I slipped up there."

"We both did, son. Never mind, these things happen. We'll just let her cool her heels for a minute. Got another carrot?"

"Yeah."

"OK, you go over and catch her, son."

Sammy soon had Two-Face back. "I think she feels sorry for her bad behaviour, Dad, and one of the reins has broken."

"Oh, that's a pity – still, at least it wasn't both of them, hey," said Johnny, patting her neck. "That's all for tonight, then."

🐎 🐎 🐎

The next time they tried Two-Face with the long-reins she behaved perfectly. She soon understood what to do, and walked easily along, while Johnny talked to her all the time.

"You need to use your voice to give her the commands for turning and standing as well, Sammy," instructed Johnny. "Get her familiar with the sounds of what you want her to do."

The long-reining continued until Two-Face was easily turning right and left when asked to, although she was not so good at standing still.

"She doesn't like to stand, does she, Dad?"

"Well, for that matter neither do you. No youngster does on the whole, too much energy," he replied. "We just need to be patient with her."

Billy had a try too, but had even less success with her, as she misbehaved when he held the reins.

"Hey! Flippin' heck!" he cried, exasperated by the filly's refusal to turn and stop.

"No, that's not working at all, Billy. You see, she's got used to Sammy, knows his voice and feels confident with him," Johnny explained. "Remember it's still early days at school for her."

Sammy realised that his friend was feeling left out, but he couldn't do anything about it while Two-Face was being trained. He would fix things later, but for now he had only the mare on his mind.

🐎 🐎 🐎

The days passed happily for Sammy, and with Dad's kind and thoughtful training, Two-Face gradually accepted the harness on her body. She learnt to turn right and left, to stop and stand, and allowed the over-check strap to be tightened one notch a day, until it was correct.

One day Johnny had a surprise for the boys. "Let's introduce her to the cart today," he said, unlocking the shed.

He manoeuvred out the two-wheeled cart, which had one seat allowing the rider to sit just behind the horse. No frills, only a simple lightweight metal frame for racing.

Billy and Sammy got hold of a shaft each and pulled the cart up to the field. Together they put the harness on Two-Face. The bridle was now complete with blinkers, so she could only see in front of her – no distractions, Johnny had said.

Then the cart was introduced to her. She sniffed it, snorted and backed away.

"That's all right, my beauty. It's not going to harm you," Sammy said gently. "You check it out all you want 'cos this little cart is the start of your racing career. It's going to be victory all the way."

Billy was stroking the other side of her neck and he softly sang, *"She's not a silly filly, she can trot faster than Sammy or Billy."*

"I'm just going to thread the shafts through the tugs and see how she feels about that, boys. Hold her firmly, Sammy."

Two-Face stood quietly as the cart was attached, then Johnny urged her to walk on. She walked hesitantly a few paces, stopped and backed up nervously. It was touch and go for a few minutes while the horse considered this new imposition. Sammy continued his reassurance by smoothing her neck and speaking softly.

Billy stroked her shoulder and sang, *"This is the start, little girl. Here's the cart, now take it for a whirl."*

And she did.

Step by step, she grew in confidence and soon she was walking along, pulling the cart. Right behind strode Johnny with the long-reins while Sammy held her bridle and told her what a good girl she was.

It took another week before Johnny felt it was the right time to sit on the seat of the cart. Two-Face began to snort and dance a little on the spot. All the harness was firmly buckled now, so it was the moment of truth for them all.

She would not walk, but pranced along, testing the limits of the harness.

Johnny finally got her trotting and took her steadily around the field. Her steps got faster as he gave her more freedom, faster and faster.

"I think she knows what's on now Sammy..." Johnny shouted, as they whizzed by, just before she broke her stride and took off at great speed.

"OH NO!" shouted Sammy.

"Well, the best ones usually have a bit of spirit," Johnny remarked with a slight smile as he and the boys took the harness off the sweating filly. "But I must admit, I didn't think Two-Face was going to stop until she reached the sea!"

"Me too, Dad, you had us worried for

a bit there 'cos, man, she can really shift, can't she!"

"Oh yes, she's got the speed. I'm looking forward to trying her out on the roads, Sammy, although there's a few more things for her to learn before that."

"Like a shot from a gun
Two- Face set off to run.
They say she's just a minor,
but she never stopped
    till she got to China!"

"Ha! Billy, you nutter," laughed Sammy. "Race you back."

They sprinted off, before Johnny could ask them to help carry some of the harness.

CHAPTER THIRTEEN

The summer rolled by. Johnny, Sammy and often Billy too, schooled Two-Face in the evenings and at weekends. She had become familiar with the harness, the lunging, long reining and the cart, so one day Johnny helped his son on to her back.

Two-Face stood calmly and accepted this new development. When Dad led her at a walk, that was not a problem either. She walked briskly, quite happy that Sammy and her supply of carrots rode astride her. So he took her alone, and after a few circles urged her to trot. She obeyed, but tossed her head a lot too.

"Keep her speed down, Sammy," Dad called.

"I'm trying, I'm trying," he shouted back, as she quickened to a canter, then suddenly launched into a series of bucks that soon had the boy on the ground.

"We should have kept her on the lunge longer, Sammy. Are you OK?" Johnny asked.

"Yeah, just that my arse hurts," he said, rubbing the affected area. "She started so cool, then suddenly got naughty."

"It's all about who's going to be boss at this stage, son. Can you face getting on board again? And try keeping her to a walk this time."

"Sure, it's her high spirits after all, isn't it? And I love that."

"Good lad, just walk her slow."

Johnny let the bridle go after a few circles, and this time Two-Face behaved herself.

Sammy made her stand, walk on, then turn left and right, all at a walking pace. He held her back with calming words and firm hands when she tossed her head and tried to dance along.

"No, girl. Walk. Stand. Easy now. Stand. Whoa girl." Sammy kept it up until she obeyed his commands perfectly.

"A lovely sight, Sammy," said Mum, when

he walked her to the house. "I'm really proud of the pair of you."

Sammy beamed. At that moment he knew he was boss.

Two-Face did not try to unseat Sammy again, apart from a few playful kicks now and then when she got excited.

"She's behaving like a proper young lady now," Cosher said admiringly on one of his visits.

"She's still a bit wild when she feels like it," Sammy replied, running his hands proudly down her gleaming neck and shoulders.

He spent a lot of time grooming her with the soft body brush he had bought. She loved that, and would nuzzle him as he brushed her coat to make it shine.

"I'll need my sunglasses to look at her soon," Cosher grinned.

Billy was not too keen to ride. "Sure I will," he said, "but later, when she's more used to having someone on her back. I'm not a limpet like you, Sammy. She'd have me off just like that!" And he jumped in the air, chanting,

"Two-Face the mighty mare,
ride her if you're able,
ride her if you dare!"

The days turned cooler and autumnal, so now they could start to try Two-Face on the roads. An early start on Sunday was best because there was hardly any traffic. Johnny rode the cart and Sammy his bike. It soon became obvious that Two-Face was at home there, and she quickly found her stride. She sped along, hooves rhythmically pounding the tarmac.

"The most awesome sound in the world," Sammy thought, peddling hard as the cart disappeared out of sight.

Eventually they returned, coming back at a steady jog, Two-Face sweating and on her toes.

"Now I'm sure she's a natural trotter, Sammy." Johnny was exhilarated. "She's taken to the road as if this is what she was born to do!"

"FANTASTIC! She was flying, Dad. She's a brilliant road horse!" Sammy was ecstatic. "Can I ride the cart a little way?"

"We can't trust cars with either you or the filly. I'm sorry, Sammy," Johnny replied.

"Does that mean I can't ever ride the

cart, Dad?"

"Not until you're older. There's so many ignorant people driving around these roads, it's far too dangerous."

"But..."

"Sammy, you know how strong your horse is. How would you stop her if she got spooked and bolted? Just think how you'd feel if there was an accident."

"Yes, I know you're right, Dad, but the field gets boring sometimes for both of us. See how she loves it out here on the road."

"True, Sammy, so I tell you what, we'll take her to the beach next weekend. There's going to be a get together of the trotters now that most of the holiday-makers have gone."

"Oh, great!" Sammy cried.

🐎 🐎 🐎

Next Sunday morning, they all set off early and headed for the beach. On board the horsebox were the whole family, including Billy, and of course, Two-Face and the cart.

It was a fine day and the three miles of

sands stretched away, looking golden in the hazy sun.

They were the first to arrive, as Johnny had got there early to give Sammy a chance to take Two-Face on his own. He was very excited. They had the filly harnessed and attached to the cart by the time Cosher arrived.

"Good day for it," he said, "and that little lady is raring to go by the look of her."

Two-Face was dancing and snorting, impatient to stretch her legs in the new surroundings.

"She can't wait, Dad." Sammy was almost prancing too.

"Just keep calm, try and hold her to a trot and don't go all the way to the far end. Pull her up about halfway. Turn her, and a steady pace back. Got that?" Johnny asked, as he walked Two-Face through the car park to the beach.

Sammy only half heard. The prospect of the long run across the sands with his horse was overwhelming. He watched her ears flicking backwards and forwards, and saw her powerful hindquarters bouncing as she stepped out right in front of him. Directly through the reins, he felt her mouth, her head, her whole will.

"It's just you and me, Two-Face," he said softly, as Johnny let go his hold on the reins. He kept her to a walk until they got clear of any people and dogs, then he urged her on.

At first the mare seemed reluctant. It was new and strange, so she trotted warily, as if the ground might suddenly subside beneath her hooves.

Sammy felt tense, ready for anything. "Come on now, Two-Face, nothing's going to hurt you, girl."

Her pace quickened as she found her stride, a fast easy trot, and soon

Sammy felt the rush of smooth speed as the filly pounded across the sands. He was aware of the waves breaking on his left, and the vast, flat beach stretching ahead, but above all, the awesome power of the speeding horse. This was IT! This was his dream come true. Flying along behind his Two-Face.

Suddenly the cliffs loomed up. Three miles had zoomed by in an instant!

"Whoa girl, whoa now."

Two-Face responded and slowed down to a prancing walk. Sammy turned her in a wide circle and headed back. Apart from breaking her stride once, everything was perfect.

"She was wonderful, we had the best run ever, Dad." Sammy was overjoyed.

"Well, you both look happy," grinned Johnny, as Billy, Cosher, Mum and the girls fussed over the boy and his horse.

Billy ran around the cart mimicking a high-stepping trot as he improvised another rap.

"The sand was all damp
For the boy and his champ.
It was Two-Face and Sammy
speedin' fast by the sea."

Other horses and carts were now arriving on the beach. It looked like a big turn-out after the summer break. Here was an opportunity to race untried horses and ease others back to fitness on the soft sands, after their weeks in the fields getting fat.

Looking over the other trotters, Sammy suddenly felt nervous. This was going to be a big test for Two-Face.

"There's some wicked lookin' trotters here, Sammy," Billy remarked.

"Yeah. I'm glad I'm not driving the cart, 'cos I don't want anything to go wrong. See that piebald over there with the red harness? He's called Magic Man and he got placed in the King of the Road race in Scotland."

"That sounds like an important race."

"It's **the** race, Billy! It might sound daft now, but to go up there and compete with Two-Face is my ultimate dream."

"You gonna take her up to Scotland?"

"Not just like that," said Sammy. "What I'm saying is that it's been my secret scheme - my biggest wish. Getting my own road horse was the start. I want her to win that race and be the fastest trotter in the country, maybe the fastest in the WORLD! I haven't told you this before, Billy 'cos nothin' was going right. But Two-Face is changing all that."

"All right, lads?" Johnny had finished talking to some friends and now he was ready to ride. "Let's see what she can do in a proper race, hey?" he said, as he jumped on the cart and took the filly over to stand by another racer.

"A mile race up to the marker," the man with a flag said.

"Get ready. Set. GO!"

Two-Face was slow off the mark and set off in pursuit of the other horses. It was difficult for the boys to see how the race was going, as the horses were half a mile away in two minutes. Yet the carts did appear to be close together.

"Come on, Billy. We'll have to go up to the finish for the next race she runs. I want to see how she looks. Cosher's up there already to clock her time."

They jogged along the sand and met Johnny on his way back.

"She's sweating, Dad."

"I'd be surprised if she wasn't."

"Well, how did she run?" Sammy asked.

"Who won?" asked Billy.

"I had some difficulty keeping her trotting. She was too excited by the other horse and forgot what she was supposed to do. I think she galloped half of the way!"

"Oh no," Sammy groaned.

"Oh, it's to be expected, it's her first experience of racing after all. First off, she went like the clappers. I tell you, Sammy, this filly has GOT IT! We've just got to keep on patiently training her. I'll run her in a couple more races yet today."

"OK, Dad. Me and Billy are going up to the finish."

Two-Face did the same thing in her next two runs, but it didn't bother Johnny. On the journey home he said, "You wait, Sammy. A few more Sundays like this and there'll be a different story to tell about young Miss Two-Face, you mark my words!"

CHAPTER FOURTEEN

The days shortened and the weather grew chilly. Two-Face was stabled now in an adapted lorry container, her winter coat clipped and her body covered in a warm rug to keep her cosy.

For the last six weeks Sammy and his Dad had been training the filly with Johnny's tailor-made exercise and feeding regime. She was given top quality food and taken out with the cart to jog along the roads every day except Monday. Sammy was always there on his bike and Billy would often accompany his friend.

Sammy watched his horse like a hawk. The way she sped along with her four legs a white blur thrilled him every day. He didn't mind that he couldn't drive her on the roads, or race her properly until he was seventeen - watching and dreaming were enough.

The road work had started at three miles a day and increased by half a mile a week until they were now doing five miles daily, which Johnny said was enough.

The trips to the beach happened every couple of weeks too, and that meant Sammy could take control of the cart and run Two-Face solo across the sands.

"Ah, the Lady Two-Face," Cosher said admiringly, as the horse and cart clattered to a halt in front of him outside the house, followed shortly after by the two boys on bikes. "She looks a million miles away from that scrawny creature you bought at Appleby."

"Too right, Cosher. She's a natural trotter and she loves it," Johnny replied, as he jumped off the cart and patted the filly's sweaty neck.

"Here's your carrots, girl," said Sammy. "Then there'll be a nice big feed in your stable after I've rubbed you down."

"How's she running, then, this fine horse of yours? What's her time?"

"Two minutes thirty over the mile, but Dad

hasn't opened her up yet, so there's a faster time to come! We've been working at her fitness for weeks now," Sammy explained, as he helped unbuckle the harness straps.

"Yes, Johnny's been keeping me up with her progress," said Cosher. "She looks hard and fit, ready for some serious competition if you ask me."

"Well, it's funny you should say that. I thought the same thing today," Johnny said, looking at his son. "I haven't told you yet, Sammy, but she clocked two fifteen on that straight bit of road after the garage today, while you were trying to catch us up!"

"Two fifteen! Wow, Dad, did you push her?"

"No. She was just cruisin', Sammy, flying along and enjoying herself."

"Yeah, I'm not surprised to hear that," Cosher said. "The word's out about her because of your beach trips. Lots of people are more than a little curious to see how she does in a proper race."

"I'll have to set something up," said Johnny thoughtfully. "With your permission of course, Sammy!"

Sammy was listening wide-eyed to the words of the two men.

He looked at his filly and said, "Well, Two-Face, what do you think?"

"What do I think?
***That** you should know!*
Just fix me a race
and watch me GO!"

"Aw, Billy, that's just what I think she'd say, you nutter," laughed Sammy.

"Yo, Billy! Yer crucial, lad," grinned Cosher.

The race was fixed for Sunday.

"What this Sunday coming?" Sammy gasped. "That's the day after tomorrow!"

"It certainly is. It only takes a few phone calls to find out who's ready to race."

"Who is ready, Dad?"

"Looks like Two-Face will be running against Britney."

"She's pretty fast, isn't she?"

"Britney's fast all right," said Cosher, "I've seen her win a few road races myself. A smart young cookie, she is."

"Not as smart as Two-Face, nor as fast, I bet," Sammy said confidently.

But later, when he was on his own with Two Face, the significance of the race to come felt terrifying. The worries rose up in his mind...

What if she loses? She might not be fast enough?

What if she doesn't want to run? She's never before raced on the road against another horse and never on a huge dual carriageway. All the car lights and strangeness might upset her.

She might freak out! She might injure herself, maybe even fatally! Racing accidents happen all the time.

Johnny! What if he should get hurt too, or worse? It happened to Billy, his Dad got crushed!

Sammy suddenly felt overwhelmed by everything. He threw his arms around his horse's neck, sobbing.

"I thought I might find you here, Sammy."
It was Johnny. "Seems like you might have a bad case of pre-race nerves, hey?"

"Sorry, Dad, I just had all sorts of stupid thoughts bangin' around my head about her, the race and you. They scared me."

"Well, it's only natural to get a bit worked up before something important, and this horse is the most important thing in your life, right?"

"She is, but so are you."

"You're worried about me too? Why's that, son?"

"Because accidents can happen, and they can be really bad."

Johnny put his arm comfortingly around Sammy's shoulders, and after a long pause he said, "You're thinking of Billy and how he lost his father. But you mustn't think that way, son. Life throws things at us all the time, more good than bad if we're lucky. If you start worrying about what might happen, where is it going to stop? You could end up staying in bed all your life!

"I appreciate your concern for me, Sammy. But I can confidently tell you that Two-Face and I are going to run as fast and as safe as possible - and don't be too surprised if we win!"

Sammy looked at his Dad's smiling face and hugged him, saying, "Yeah, Dad, I was only making sure."

🐎 🐎 🐎

Billy came over the next day so he and Sammy could spend time with Two-Face before the race. They groomed her, then rode her around the field for a while to stretch her legs. "No exertion or training today," Johnny had said.

It was a wintry day, cold and drizzly, so the boys chilled out with computer games until an early bedtime. The alarm was set for 4.45am!

🐎 🐎 🐎

"Hey, Billy!" called Sammy at 5.15 next morning. "Hurry up! We're all ready 'cept for you! Two-Face is loaded in the horsebox and Dad's in the cab already. He says he's goin' without you if you don't come now."

"Yeah, yeah, OK. I'm just looking for my other sock." Billy sounded S-L-O-W.

"Here, put this pair on, Billy, we gotta GO!"

Sammy pushed Billy up into the cab where Johnny already had the engine running, and they moved off before the door was shut.

"It's dry, lads, that's good for the race. Bit nippy though, hey?" said Johnny briskly.

"I'm freezing," Billy said rubbing his hands together.

"Will the cold affect Two-Face, Dad?"

"No, Sammy, she'll have enough to think about. The heater's on, Billy, but we'll be there before the cab's had a chance to warm up."

They soon pulled up beside another horsebox, and there were also lots of pick-up trucks and cars parked near the slip-road to the by-pass. Sammy wondered what the filly would make of the strange landscape of these wide roads illuminated by eerie orange lights. Yet she was used to street lighting now, because it was often dark when they returned home from of the miles of road jogging.

"Oh there you are at last." It was Cosher, his face partly obscured by a big scarf. "Got some big news for you lot!"

"What's that then?" Johnny asked.

"Britney's been pulled out of the race and you'll never guess who's running against your young star."

"WHO?" Sammy and Johnny spoke as one.

"Steely Dan."

"STEELY DAN!" they chorused again.

"But he's really famous," gasped Sammy.

"Famous and fast," Johnny said slowly. "Now I'm nervous."

Cosher came closer and in hushed tones said, "The official line is that Britney's lame, but unofficially they say Mr 'Big Money' Locke, - Steely's owner, - has heard about Two-Face and wants to give Steely some exercise against her!"

Johnny listened intently to this information. Then, pulling open the bolts of the horsebox, he said, "Well, there's nothing like jumping in the deep end. Let's get to it!"

🐎 🐎 🐎

Sammy heard Steely Dan approaching before he saw him, the sounds of one of the fastest set of hooves in the country. He came alongside Two-Face and his driver had a few words with Johnny, who was also on his cart and ready for action.

"Cor, that is some horse," Billy said.

Standing a good hand taller than Two-Face and more muscular, Steely looked massive.

"Awesome," Sammy whispered. "Come on, Billy, they're almost ready. We must get on board Cosher's pick-up."

The boys quickly climbed into the open back and the 4x4 rolled forward. There was a similar vehicle driving alongside, with one of Dad's mates ready to film the race.

Together they drove slowly down the slip-road, hazard lights flashing, followed by the two prancing horses, steam blowing out of their nostrils in the cold air. About 50 metres behind them was a procession of cars, headlights blazing.

Sammy was so wound-up by all that was happening, he suddenly felt ill.

"I'm gonna be sick, Billy."

"Not over me, Sammy... Hey! We're away."

The two leading vehicles pulled out on to the dual carriageway, which was blocked to other traffic by three stationary cars parked across it, also with their lights flashing.

The race was of course an unauthorised event. But as it was run at 6am in the morning, it only held up the traffic for about ten minutes. And it did not happen often enough to get the local constabulary's hackles up.

The excited horses accelerated in unison, their powerful hindquarters like pistons, driving them forward.

It was a breathtaking sight. Sammy and Billy gripped the back of the pick-up and watched the racers from in front. Side by side the trotters competed, their outlines illuminated by the pursuing cars' headlights. Sparks flew from their hooves as they hammered the road.

"THIRTY-THREE MPH!" yelled the man in the back of the other vehicle.

This was very fast. Could Two-Face keep it up for two miles?

Could Johnny keep her balanced and fluent in her gait? That was the most crucial thing

he had to do, sit still and keep hold of her head. Her legs would do the rest.

"Steely Dan's getting in front," cried Billy.

"Oh no," Sammy groaned.

"Come on, Two-Face! COME ON, GIRL!" he shouted, almost beside himself
with anxiety.

Billy sang loudly,

"RUN, Two Face, RUN,
the race is almost DONE!
Steely you can BEAT,
and make us all feel SWEET!"

"She's coming back, she's coming back! Come on, Two-Face! COME ON!" The boys jumped up and down as they shrieked encouragement to the battling horse. "YOU CAN DO IT, GIRL!"

"We're slowing, it's over. Who won, Sammy? Was it her?"

"I don't know, Billy, I just know she's fantastic! Seeing her race, seeing that POWER! I haven't ever felt like this. Isn't she amazing?"

"Massively, mammothly, mega amazing, Sammy. I'm SO glad you're my friend!"

"Aw Billy, you crack me up."

The car horns honked their approval as the procession of horses, carts and vehicles quickly left the big road and entered the quiet back lanes. The traffic that had been delayed by the race changed up a gear and speeded on its way.

Race over.

🐎 🐎 🐎

Sammy couldn't wait to hug his horse when they got back to the horsebox.

"Oh, you were wonderful, girl, and you too, Dad," Sammy said, after burying his face in Two-Face's sweaty and salty neck.

"She's special all right, Sammy, to keep up with Steely. Well, what will she be capable off in the future?" Johnny said, his voice hoarse and raspy from shouting encouragement during the race.

"I'll tell you what she'll do, Dad, run in the King of the Road! That was my dream and she's going to make it come true. She's gonna win that race!"

"Whoa hey, Sammy, aim for the top, boy," said Cosher appreciatively. "She clocked 33mph at one point back there, so she's well eligible."

Just then Steely Dan's owner appeared.

"Hello," he said, "I'd like to congratulate your horse and driver on a fine race against my Steely Dan. Obviously he wasn't on very good form but it was an excellent contest, and I am quite happy with the result being a draw."

"A superb race," said Johnny. "We could match them again in a few weeks if you think your trotter was off-form. What do you think, Sammy? This, Mr Locke, is my son, and the owner of Two-Face."

"Any time your horse is ready, then Two-Face will be too," Sammy replied, patting his filly's shoulder.

"Ah, so you are the owner of this young horse, Sammy. Well, I have a proposition I would like to put to you. I think that in the right hands she could have great potential and I would like to offer you a substantial sum of money for her. £10,000 in fact. Cash, of course."

There was a shocked silence amongst the group. Nobody said a word. Then Two Face stamped her feet and snorted loudly.

"There's your answer, Mr Locke. She says NO WAY!" said Sammy with the biggest smile on his face, as he turned to face the man. "She IS in the right hands, and I totally agree with her, because she's the finest horse in all of England and you don't have enough money to pay her price!"

Everyone except Mr Locke cheered.

Sammy grinned at Billy, then buried his face in the mare's sweaty neck and mane.

"King of the Road, here we come, Two-Face," he whispered, and the mare nickered softly in reply.

Caroline Binch has a life-long love of horses
and a respectful admiration for the peoples
of marginalised cultures and alternative lifestyles.
She got to know a Gypsy Romany family through
contacts from Cornwall Council's excellent
Equality and Diversity Services for Children,
Schools and Families. She thinks Appleby Fair
in Cumbria, which she hopes to visit annually,
is an unmissable experience.

Caroline illustrated the best-selling picture
books *Amazing Grace* and *Grace and Family*
by Mary Hoffman. *Gregory Cool*, which she
wrote and illustrated, was shortlisted for the
Kate Greenaway Medal and *Since Dad Left* won
a United Kingdom Literacy Association Award.
Her other books for Frances Lincoln include
Christy's Dream, Silver Shoes and *Down by
the River* (with Grace Hallworth). Caroline
lives by the sea in West Cornwall.